PULSE OF THE HEARTLAND

PULSE OF THE HEARTLAND

BY

MELINDA CROSS

MILLS & BOON LIMITED
ETON HOUSE   18–24 PARADISE ROAD
RICHMOND   SURREY   TW9 1SR

First published in Great Britain 1990
by Mills & Boon Limited

© Melinda Cross 1990

Australian copyright 1990
Philippine copyright 1990
Large Print edition 1990

ISBN 0 263 12371 5

Set in Times Roman 16 on 17¼ pt.
16-9009-50080 C

Printed and bound in Great Britain by
William Clowes, Beccles, Suffolk.

CHAPTER ONE

EMILY could smell the gardenias even before she was halfway down the narrow steps that led from her apartment to the flower shop below. In another week the glossy green plants would be in full bloom, sending their sweet, exotic fragrance all the way up the stairs to perfume her living quarters. It was one of the things she loved most about her little apartment, hot as it had been lately—it always smelled like a garden.

With efficient movements that had become automatic over the years, she unlocked the door at the bottom of the stairs, entered the back workroom, and snatched a green cotton overall from a hook on the wall. It was one more unwelcome garment in the unseasonable May heat, buttoning up the front from knees to neck, but at least it allowed her the freedom of wearing abbreviated shorts and a skimpy tank-top beneath—an outfit that would have raised every brow in the tiny Minnesota farming town of Random, no matter how high the temperature rose. It just wasn't the sort of thing they would expect to see on the body of their sedate, conservative florist. As a matter of fact, there were times when Emily wondered if anyone ever credited her with having a body at all.

She smoothed her closely cut blonde hair back behind her ears, thinking that it was almost time to have it trimmed again. Wispy, frivolous bangs were threatening to brush her pale brows, and frivolity was one thing she simply could not abide, especially when it came to the way she looked. For all of her twenty-seven years, Emily Swenson's appearance had reflected her philosophy and her life—busy, hard-working, and earnest. She kept her hair painfully short to save the minutes a longer length would have required, her clothing simple, and her make-up to a minimum. That any trace of vulnerability managed to survive such a presentation was a credit to her classically feminine features — a small, straight nose, a full, irrepressibly sensual mouth, and large, thickly lashed eyes. Mossy green eyes, 'just about the same colour as the algae on my stock pond', old Martin Tollefson had told her once in a backhanded compliment.

She smiled every time she remembered that, and this morning was no different, but even a smile did little to soften the underlying sternness in her face, a sternness conceived in her farming heritage, and honed by the growing years she'd spent working side by side with her father on the family farm. While other young girls had been giggling at slumber parties and exchanging the baffling secrets of burgeoning femininity, Emily had been tossing hay bales and ploughing fields, developing a decidedly unfeminine musculature. It hadn't been much of a childhood for a young girl — forever trying to match the work output of the sons her parents had never had — but Emily had no regrets. It had made her strong.

Was it attitude that shaped the way you looked, or the other way around? she wondered as she peered into the tiny mirror nailed to the back of the door. Whatever the cause, she had earned the somehow cruel nickname of Earnest Emily way back in school, and, although she hated it, even she had to admit that the label was appropriate. She *was* earnest, and so she *looked* earnest, and if the truth be told there wasn't anything wrong with that. Besides, she remembered with some satisfaction, no one had ever called her that to her face—at least not more than once.

Remembering the old nickname irritated her, and she jerked her head away from the mirror and turned to survey the small room, hands on hips.

Tall, glass-doored coolers lined two walls, and a series of huge wooden work-tables took up the rest of the floor space. The end cooler was literally stuffed with deep purple irises, and it was there that she headed first, removing an enormous armful that she cradled like a baby. Her nose automatically buried itself in the bouquet, searching for a fragrance that she knew refrigeration had already destroyed. It didn't seem right, somehow, that such a beautiful flower should be robbed of its scent; but then it didn't seem right that such a beautiful flower should be associated with sadness, either. And yet that was the way it was in the farming states of America's Midwest—the iris and the gladiolus were traditional funeral flowers, seldom used for any other purpose, because the association with death was so strong.

'And that's too bad,' Emily murmured aloud, almost feeling sorry for the flowers she held, because they were destined to celebrate sorrow, never joy, and that was a poor fate for anything—even a flower.

She shifted the bouquet to one arm and bumped her hip against the swinging door that led to the shop proper. Whenever she could, she preferred to work out here, standing at the long formica counter that ran the length of the back wall, facing the plate-glass windows that looked out on to

Random's Main Street. There were dust circles on the windows already, she noticed with a frown, even though she'd just washed them two days earlier.

The shop was an extension of Emily's ordered mind, with cylindrical stands of white plastic for displaying plants and pottery, stark white walls, and crisp green and white tiles on the floor. One's first impression of the shop was cleanliness; the second was coolness—a decided advantage during heat spells like this one.

She laid the irises down on the counter, then went to unlock the front door and flip over the 'open' sign.

Less than ten minutes later the little bell over the door tinkled and Emily glanced up from the spray she was arranging. A tall, raw-boned man entered, whipped a battered straw hat from his head, and approached the counter with that tell-tale shuffle peculiar to farmers in this part of the country. He was as out of place in the shop as any man could have been, in faded blue overalls, heavy boots, and a long-sleeved shirt that made Emily hot just to look at it. A gloriously thick shock of pure white hair topped his head, and his face was as weathered and wrinkled as old leather. Bright blue eyes winked out from the folds of ageing skin around them. 'Morning, Em.'

Emily placed one hand on her chest and feigned surprise. 'Martin Tollefson in a flower shop? I don't believe it!'

He ducked his head with a sheepish grin and turned his hat in his hands. 'Don't think I've been through that door since you opened this place. No need, really. Seemed simpler just to call.'

Emily flashed a brief smile across the counter, then looked back down at her work. Every year Martin ordered a dozen anniversary roses for his wife, but always by phone. 'I heard your whole family is gathering for the celebration this year, Martin.'

'Every one of the kids will be here,' he nodded proudly. 'Bobby and his brood are coming up from Tennessee, Sarah's coming from California, and the twins are flying in from New York. First time in years we'll have all the grandchildren under the roof at one time, and Harriet's just about fit to be tied, she's so excited. Don't know how she'll get through the next couple of weeks, waiting for it.'

'June the fifth, right?'

'Hey,' Martin sounded pleased, 'you remembered.' There was a brief silence, then his boots shuffled self-consciously on the tiled floor. 'I want it to be special this year, Emily.' His voice quivered with a timidity that made her look up curiously. Martin Tollefson was never timid, any more than any other farmer in this township. Certainty, pride, dominance—these were the earmarks of the breed of man who worked this land; timidity was the sole province of their wives.

'Fifty years married to the same woman,' he went on, his expression almost wistful. 'It ought to be special. It still has to be roses, of course. Harriet does love her anniversary roses, but I thought if I gave you enough lead time you might be able to get in some of those tiny ones, so I could put a bunch in every room.'

Emily paused in her work and looked at the old man with something like wonder. Harriet Tollefson was as surely under her husband's thumb as any other farm wife in Random. Relationships were biscuit-cutter duplicates out here...and yet...there was something odd in the old man's voice when he spoke his wife's name. Something undeniably romantic, and very nearly reverent. Extraordinary, she mused. Fifty years, and he still wanted to fill the house with roses for his wife. Maybe the Tollefsons did have something different; something a little more special than all the other farming couples who made up the populace of Random.

'I'll take care of it, Martin,' she said quietly, and something in her gaze made the old seamed face colour from the bottom up, as if they'd just shared something extraordinarily intimate.

'Well,' he hedged, looking around uncomfortably, his gaze finally settling on the spray of irises she was arranging. 'Guess I probably didn't pick the best day to drop in. Looks like you got your hands full.' He nodded down at the flowers. 'Those for Art Simon?'

Emily nodded, her expression properly sombre.

'Well, he was a good man. The town'll miss him. Too bad he had to go so young.'

She had to suppress a smile as Martin turned and left the shop. Art Simon had been a month past his ninety-fifth birthday when he'd died three days ago. Maybe when she was seventy-eight, as Martin was now, ninety-five would sound young to her, too.

She spent the rest of the morning alone in the shop, putting together the many arrangements that had been ordered for Art's funeral. One by one, vases and sprays and bouquets of irises and gladioli took their place by the front door, waiting for Sam Beckett, the funeral director, to pick them up. She was just tying together the last bunch when the bell over the door jangled for the second time that morning.

'You're early, Sam,' she said without looking up, 'but this is the last one. Ready in a minute.'

There was the soft, muffled squeak of tennis shoes coming to an abrupt stop on the tiles just inside the door, and she knew then that it wasn't Sam. Sam never wore anything but proper shoes.

Emily raised her head with the expression of polite interest she reserved for people she didn't know well, and squinted towards the door. The shadow of a man stood against the backlight of the glass, frozen for a moment in a posture that made her think of a tennis player waiting to receive a serve.

'Can I help you?'

His head tipped at her voice, as if to hear her better. 'Well I'll be damned,' he said after a moment. 'It's you.' There was something familiar about the deep, mellow voice, but she couldn't place it.

'I beg your pardon?'

'It *is* Earnest Emily, isn't it?'

Her face stilled, then she lifted her chin defensively. No one had called her that since

those awkward, painful school-days. It irritated her to suddenly hear the nickname
again, as if her thoughts of the morning had
somehow conjured it up.

'I'm busy,' she said shortly, fussing with the
flowers on the counter, completely forgetting
that whoever he was he was a potential
customer.

'You were always busy, Emily.'

Damn, she knew that voice. She *knew* she
did. It snaked across the room like oil on a
hot skillet, slick and sure and maddeningly
deep, a curious cross between mockery and
playfulness...

Her head jerked up and her eyes narrowed.
'Nick?'

As if he'd only been waiting to be recognised, he snapped from immobility and approached the counter with that jaunty,
confident stride that was so uniquely his; she
had never to this day seen one remotely like
it. Thank heaven. She'd never liked Nicholas
Simon. Not in gradeschool, not in high
school, and she probably wouldn't like him

as an adult, either. He'd always been in the centre of that high-popularity clique of star athletes and giddy cheerleaders, and even from a distance she'd always thought he exemplified the shallowness of those who worried more about the location of the next party than the harsh realities of life.

And then, of course, there'd been that horrible scene right after the graduation ceremony. Right in front of the whole damn town, on a dare, no less, the most popular boy in school had grabbed the notoriously unapproachable Earnest Emily, and kissed her smack on the mouth. He'd probably forgotten the incident seconds after it had happened, but she still bristled with humiliation every time she recalled it.

She repressed those feelings out of consideration as he bounced towards her, even though she found it irritating that his step could be so light, today of all days. It was *his* grandfather who had died, after all. He could have at least had the decency to temper that cocky walk of his and *try* to look mournful.

In a startlingly neat hop he was perched on the counter, leaning towards her on the rigid brace of his right arm, one corner of his mouth lifted in a smile that seemed to mock the world. If his sudden closeness hadn't been enough to fluster her, his clothing—or lack of it—certainly was.

He wore faded, expensive jeans that lay across his thighs like a second skin, and a tank-top much like the one she was hiding beneath her florist coat—only he wasn't hiding his, or anything else, for that matter.

The powerful shoulders of a fully matured man rose from the slender black straps of the shirt, and, beneath it, the well-defined muscles of his chest pressed their outline into the thin fabric. He was broader, thicker, even taller than she remembered him, and the naked arm braced on the counter looked massive and masculine next to her own.

'Emily, Emily, Emily.' He shook his head slowly, and his thick, light hair echoed the movement a fraction of a beat later, quivering over his brow like the lazy waves of a golden ocean of wheat. There was new breadth to his square jaw, and Emily noted the shadow of a beard that would be several shades darker than his sun-bleached hair.

I'll bet empty-headed females *still* fall all over him, she thought with disdain, feeling wonderfully superior to be above such petty attractions.

As he watched her study him, a network of tiny lines appeared next to eyes the colour of a summer sky, eyes that still glittered with boyish mischief. Such eyes had no business in the face of a mature man, she decided.

'What on earth are you doing back here, Emily?'

'I'm not "back",' she said crisply, intent on letting him know that the exercise of his infamous charm would be lost on her. 'I never left.'

'You're kidding? You stayed in Random, all this time? You didn't go to college?'

'Obviously not.' She concentrated on aligning the flower stems, her lips primly pursed, her eyes narrowed.

'But that's crazy. You could have gone to any college in the country with your grades. Why on earth would you stay hidden away in a place like Random?'

She raised her head with a look of chilling condescension. 'I happen to like Random. It's my home.'

It was a stock answer, of course, and not quite the truth. The truth was, she wasn't sure why she stayed in this little one-horse town, with the lure of a city like Minneapolis less than two hundred miles away. Granted, there had been her mother's illness; but even Emily knew that was just an excuse. She hadn't made a bee-line for the city after the crisis was over, now had she? And that had been nearly nine years ago.

'I know what you mean,' Nick murmured, and she had to concentrate to remember what they'd been talking about. 'I regret leaving Random every time I come back.' He shrugged lightly. 'Don't know what it is, really. The land, maybe; the people, more likely. All those good old-fashioned country values you can't seem to find anywhere else.'

Emily grunted softly as she straightened a folded leaf on a particularly long stem. Country values, indeed. The people who lived here were always touting those, as if they went hand in hand with open fields and country air. 'No fifty per cent divorce rate in Random,' they were fond of saying, and Emily sometimes wondered if they believed broken marriages were a contagious disease of some sort, a city-bred virus that couldn't survive the crop-filled plains. She knew better, of course. If Random and other farm towns like it never saw divorce, it was because the women out here were born and bred to bow down to men, to accept a subservient role, as if that were the way Nature had intended it.

It was typical, she thought, that a man like Nick would see Random, a town filled with obedient women, as paradise.

'If you liked it here that much, why did you leave?' she asked sharply.

He sighed and shrugged, looking around the shop. 'I wanted to be a doctor. Big city practice, big city money, big city life...all the standard dreams, but now that I've got them...' He let the sentence trail away in a sheepish grin. 'Is this shop yours?'

'That's right.'

He stroked his chin thoughtfully with one finger as his jaw jutted forward. 'I suppose that makes sense. You always did love flowers, didn't you?'

She frowned, wondering how he had ever known such a thing.

He saw her expression and smiled. 'The school bus always dropped you off before me. I'd watch out of the back window as we pulled away, and every day during the summer you'd stop in the ditch at the end of your driveway to smell those wild black-eyed Susans, remember?'

Emily blinked at him, astounded that he had ever noticed—that *anyone* had ever noticed.

He chuckled at her astonishment. 'Used to drive me crazy. You were so tough in those days, so hard-nosed; no time for friends, no time for fun...' he paused and shook his head, remembering '. . . but you always found time to stop and look at those stupid flowers. I couldn't figure it out. It was such a *feminine* thing to do.'

Emily bristled a little. 'And in all other respects I wasn't the least bit feminine, right?'

His smile was almost apologetic. 'There weren't many girls in our class who could toss eighty-pound hay bales as far as a man. And speaking of that, who's doing all the muscle work for your dad, now that you're in business for yourself?'

'I can *still* toss my fair share of hay bales,' she said tightly, thinking that she could probably toss Nick Simon through a plate-glass window, too. 'But he doesn't need much help any more. He cut way back on farming when Mom got sick.'

His eyes were suddenly serious. 'Your mom is sick?'

She looked down at her work and shook her head impatiently. 'Not any more. She had a bout of meningitis the year we graduated——'

'Dear lord,' he whispered. 'Meningitis.'

'But she's all right now. Not as strong as she used to be, but otherwise OK.'

'She must have been laid up for a long time.'

'Over a year.'

He looked off to the side and shook his head. 'I'm sorry, Emily. I didn't know. It must have been a hard time.'

She lifted one shoulder in a dismissive shrug, then glanced up sharply when she heard his chuckle.

'Earnest Emily...still as tough as ever, aren't you?'

'Don't call me that!' she snapped with more vehemence than she had intended, her chin jutting forward like a spear aimed at his face.

'Hey,' he said quietly, raising both hands in surrender. His brows came together in the frown that had created the faint vertical line above his nose. 'Take it easy. It wasn't meant as an insult.' He cocked his head and looked at her for a moment, then added, 'Ever.'

Emily closed her eyes briefly and sighed, then reached beneath the counter for a length of violet florist's paper. She began to wrap the last bouquet of irises, forgetting that their destination didn't require it. 'I didn't mean to snap,' she mumbled down at the flowers. 'I just always hated that name.'

'Then I won't call you that,' he said in that same quiet tone. For some reason, she found an earnest Nick Simon far more disturbing than an ebullient one, but fortunately it wasn't a condition that lasted long. With an abruptness that gave her a start, he hopped down to the floor and faced her across the counter with an impudent grin the years hadn't altered. He certainly didn't look much like a doctor, she thought. Doctors were supposed to be dignified, weren't they? 'We'll start over,' he proclaimed, straightening to his full, considerable height, tipping his head in a mockery of a polite greeting. 'Well, if it isn't Emily Swenson, smartest girl in Random High. How are you, Emily? Nice to see you again. It's been almost ten years, hasn't it?' Suddenly the flip recitation stopped, and his eyes narrowed slightly. 'My God,' he whispered, 'I'd almost forgotten that spectacular figure of yours.'

Emily's eyes widened when she saw he was gazing openly at her bustline, and she felt the sudden, mortifying rush of colour to her face.

His smile was more like a leer, and for a moment she hardly knew how to react. He was mocking her, just as he'd mocked her with that impudent kiss ten years ago, but this time he'd made a mistake. She wasn't the naïve, gullible girl she'd been then. Now she knew how to strike back.

'Too bad you couldn't get back to see your grandfather *before* he died,' she sniped viciously, paying him back for a transgression that was ten years old.

His brows shot up instantly, and, although his smile remained stiffly in place, all the humour seemed to bleed from his eyes, leaving them a much lighter shade of blue. 'My, my,' he drawled. 'Age has certainly sharpened your claws, hasn't it?'

Emily frowned hard and looked down, regretting the cruelty of her words, even if he *had* deserved to hear them. 'I shouldn't have said that,' she muttered sullenly. 'Your relationship with your grandfather was none of my business, and even if——'

'Your hair's a lot shorter.'

While she was still trying to recover from the sudden change of subject, his forearms popped into her field of vision, bracing his weight against the counter, and she found herself staring at them as if she'd never seen a man's arms before. They were deeply tanned, the ridge of muscle running from wrist to elbow frosted with tiny golden hairs.

'I like it, all slicked back like that,' he went on, as if his grandfather's funeral, up-and-coming main attraction, had never been mentioned. 'It's very businesslike; very no-nonsense.' His mouth curved lazily. 'Very masculine. But the body gives you away, Emily. You couldn't hide it then, and you can't hide it now.'

Her lips pressed together like a door slamming shut. He hadn't changed a bit. He was still hustling anything with a pulse, still supremely confident that there wasn't a woman alive who could resist his charms.

'I told you before, Nick,' she said coldly, 'I'm busy. Now, if you want something, fine. If you don't, I suggest you go somewhere and get ready for your grandfather's funeral.'

He remained motionless for a moment, studying her face with quiet amusement, then he pushed away from the counter and straightened. It unnerved Emily a little to have to look up to meet his gaze. 'You have daisies?' he asked.

'Of course I have daisies, but if you're thinking of the funeral——'

'How many do you have on hand?'

The question caught her off guard. 'Well...I don't know. I use them for filler, mostly. No one actually orders *daisies* for anything, especially around here. The fields are full of them——'

'How many?' he repeated, and for the first time his voice was firm.

'Five dozen. Maybe six.'

'Good,' he nodded brusquely. 'Wrap them up and send them over with those sorry things.' His head jerked towards the mass of deep purple irises by the door.

She opened her mouth to protest, then checked his eyes and changed her mind. 'All right. What shall I put on the card?'

His face shifted instantly to its old mocking expression. 'Card? Now who on earth, Emily, would read the card?' Then he turned away and started towards the door.

Emily watched him go with a disapproving scowl, thinking how perfectly awful, how disrespectful it was to order something as gay and common as daisies for his own grandfather's funeral. Still, when his hand reached for the doorknob, she felt compelled to call after him. 'Nick?'

He froze, then looked over his shoulder.

'I liked your grandfather,' she said quietly.

'Thank you, Emily. So did I.'

CHAPTER TWO

IN A town of less than five hundred souls, almost everyone was at the very least a nodding acquaintance of everyone else. That was the extent of Emily's knowledge of Nicholas Simon's grandfather—she had known him well enough to exchange a greeting if they met on the street, but that was all. Still, in the long list of all Emily's nodding acquaintances in Random, Art Simon had occupied a special place. Without really knowing him at all, even she had realised that there was something special about the elderly gentleman. There would have to be, she thought wryly, for him to take in and raise an orphaned grandson like Nick.

Sprightly even in his nineties, Art had always been totally self-sufficient, still working a small section of his large farm right up until the day he died—on his tractor, she remembered, thinking that he would have wanted it that way.

In some parts of the country a man his age still working would have been a miracle—in the grain belt of the Midwest it was simply the way things were. A man worked until his last day, because the relationship with the land was something you didn't just turn your back on when you reached the age of sixty-five. It was a part of you, all the way to the grave.

But it wasn't just Art Simon's longevity that had touched the untouchable Emily. 'You're going to be a real beauty one day,' he'd told her at a community picnic when she was twelve and gangling and painfully shy, and even though she'd huffed and blustered, mortified in typical tomboy fashion that her looks had been noticed at all, she had never forgotten the kindness of his words.

She *had* liked him, she thought, as she dressed for the three o'clock funeral—just as she'd told Nick this morning—and then she felt a rush of sadness stronger than she had ever expected, because she wished she had known him better, and now her chance was gone.

Stupid, she derided herself as she pulled on an impossibly hot black dress and slipped into low heels. You barely knew the man, and you're more upset at his passing than his own grandson. The reminder of Nick's callousness made her angry all over again. Big city doctor with big city schedule or not, the least he could have done was spend more time with the old man. Although she'd heard a few times that Nick had visited—on holidays mostly—as far as she knew he had left Random and his grandfather ten years ago, with barely a backward glance.

'Ingrate,' she muttered aloud, beating back the uncomfortable, inexplicable grief for one stranger with contempt for another.

She buttoned her dress up to its high collar, jerked the belt tight, slicked her short light hair sideways up and away from her face, then left the stifling confines of her apartment.

Nick wasn't at the church. Everyone else in Random had come, including her own parents—she could see her father's broad shoulders and her mother's tiny form far ahead in one of the front pews—but Art Simon's only relative was conspicuously absent.

In spite of his apparent nonchalance earlier in the shop, Emily was still shocked by this gross breach of etiquette, this appalling lack of respect for the man who had raised him.

Later, after the last sombre words had been spoken in the town's lonely cemetery, she watched as they piled dozens and dozens of bright white and yellow daisies high over Art Simon's grave-site. They looked impossibly, irreverently gay, and entirely unsuitable in the gathering of black-clad mourners.

'Emily,' her mother's soft murmur came from directly behind her, and Emily's forced smile was automatic as she turned and bent at the waist to kiss her mother's cheek.

Such a tiny, helpless woman, she thought with a sigh, gazing into the green eyes so like her own. Totally subservient to her husband, in a way Emily would never be subservient to any man, by God; and yet so clearly adapted to that kind of existence.

Strong father, acquiescent mother—the standard description for farm-country marriages. Carl and Mary Swenson's roles had been defined long before Emily's birth, and she had decided early which example to follow.

Mary Swenson's brief, terribly debilitating illness had polarised the man-woman positions even further, of course. For the entire year that she had been bedridden, her husband had been fiercely protective, the epitome of masculine strength, coddling and cherishing his wife as if she'd been a helpless doll of some sort. The worst part was that, although the illness made it more visible, that was basically the way they had always related to one another. Emily idolised her father, and felt a tender, protective sort of love for her mother, but she still found the woman's willing submission to male dominance faintly repulsive. *She'd* certainly never fall victim to such archaic role-playing.

'How are you, Emily? You look tired.'

'Maybe just a little. The shop had a lot of orders for today.'

She looks so fragile in black, Emily thought; more like a toy woman than a real one. The green eyes were Mary Swenson's only genetic contribution to her tall, strong, fair-haired daughter. Her own hair was crow-wing black, curved softly around a china-pale face with petite, delicate features and a tiny rosebud mouth.

'You need to get away from the store for a while, dear. Why don't I take over for a week or so——?'

Emily was shaking her head before her mother could finish the sentence. 'Don't be silly. You have your hands full at the farm. Besides, what would I do?'

Her mother's face tightened a little, and something in the green eyes flashed. 'Go to the city. Stay in a ritzy hotel. Shop all day and dance all night. Have a little fun, for a change. Meet some new people...'

'A man, you mean. A nice, strong man who'll marry me and take care of me for the rest of my life.'

Mary looked at her steadily. 'I didn't say that.'

'Not this time,' Emily conceded, remembering all the times she *had* said it. Her mother refused to believe any woman could be happy outside the demanding circle of a man's attention. 'I keep telling you, Mom. I'm not like you. I don't want to be taken care of. And if I ever marry it will be to a man who understands that.'

She sighed and glanced around at the thinning crowd, looking for a way to change the subject. 'Poor Art,' she said finally, an undercurrent of sharp disapproval in her tone. 'His own grandson didn't even come.'

She could feel her mother's gaze on her profile. 'I doubt that Art noticed. Besides, funerals just aren't Nicky's style.'

'"Nicky"?' Emily parodied. 'I didn't know you knew him.'

Her mother turned to look back at the grave and shrugged mildly. 'Art talked about him all the time. I feel I know him.'

Emily's mouth turned down. 'He came into the shop this morning. He actually ordered all those daisies.'

Mary's smile was spontaneous, and not the least bit disapproving. Disgruntled that her mother found neither the daisies nor Nick's absence disturbing, Emily turned away and pretended an interest in the clusters of people who were finally moving away towards their cars. She caught sight of her father out on the road, leaning against the dusty side of his pick-up truck, waiting impatiently for his wife. He raised a long arm when he caught Emily's eye, signalling that he wanted to leave. Occasionally death intruded on the placid existence of Random's farming residents, but it never stopped life for long.

'Father wants you,' she said sullenly, knowing that those three words would always produce an immediate obedient response. Carl Swenson beckoned, his wife followed. Always.

'I suppose,' Mary sighed, turning to give her daughter a quick hug before she left. 'You know your father. An hour away from the fields is too much. Don't forget. You're coming out for dinner on Friday.'

'Six o'clock,' Emily promised, then watched her mother walk away towards the man who controlled her life—the man who *was* her life. Never, never, never, she vowed, would she let herself become so humiliatingly enslaved to a man. If that kind of subservience was the price one paid for love, then she didn't want any part of it.

She sighed and pushed her hands back through her short-cropped hair, wondering for the millionth time if perhaps she shouldn't move to the city, where the old-fashioned, sharp divisions between men and women had died an ignominious death long ago.

Suddenly just being in the town's peaceful, tree-shaded cemetery made her feel trapped, and she strode briskly across the dried, clipped grass to her car. Her low heels sank into the sod, as if the place itself was a malign presence that wanted to keep her there forever.

*   *   *

'Ehh-mih-lee! Oh, Ehh-mih-lee!'

Her eyes flew open, and for a moment she lay paralysed in the total blackness of her bedroom, her palms pressed tight against her chest, wondering what had shattered her sleep so abruptly. She heard the gentle whisper of the curtains at the open window, the muted tick of her bedside clock, and, off in the distance, the barking of a dog. Other than that, nothing.

She released the breath she'd been holding and closed her eyes.

'Ehh-mih-lee!'

This time she shot out of bed, her heart pounding, and stood next to it with her green eyes wide and frightened. When the sound was repeated yet again, she recognised it as a human voice, and her whole body sagged in relief. In the next second it straightened with indignation. Kids, probably, caterwauling beneath her window on a dare.

Her face tight with irritation, she padded across the room towards the window, the wooden floor deliciously cool beneath her bare feet. She draped the curtain in front of the thin cotton nightie that barely hung to her thighs, and peered out and down.

'You!' Her lips formed the word almost inaudibly as she saw Nicholas Simon a full storey below, his head tipped back on his shoulders to look up, a lop-sided grin showing the white of his teeth in the darkness.

'Emily! Hi!' he bellowed delightedly when he saw her, and she clamped a forefinger to her lips.

'What are you doing?' she hissed down at him. 'Do you want to wake the whole town?'

His head started to shake in a slow roll, the foolish grin still in place, and Emily's eyes narrowed suspiciously. Now she could see that his wide-legged stance was not pure arrogance; it was an attempt to counter unsteadiness.

'Get away from here!' she whispered. 'Go home!'

'Nope.' His head was still shaking, throwing his hair back and forth across his brow. 'I came to pay a visit. I came to see my old schoolmate, Earnest Emily, and I'm not leaving until I do.'

Her lips pursed in consternation. 'You're drunk,' she accused him, but that only prompted an even broader grin.

'Could be, could be. But, drunk or not, I'm going to stand down here and shout until you let me in!' His voice grew louder and louder with every word, and Emily jerked back from the window in alarm. He really *was* going to wake the whole town.

'What do you want?'

'I told you. I just came to pay a visit. It's a courtesy call.' The word 'courtesy' was the first he had stumbled over, and to Emily that seemed incredibly appropriate. 'Not very hospitable, are you, Earnest Emily? Least you could do is invite an old friend in for coffee. 'Specially one in my condition. You wouldn't want me to *drive home drunk, would you*?'

'All right, all right!' she hissed, panicking because he was shouting so loudly. 'Just a minute!'

She snatched her short cotton robe from the chair in the corner, shrugged into it, jerked the belt tight around her waist, and opened her bedroom door so hard that it slammed against the wall.

She muttered continually under her breath as she stomped through her dark apartment, down the narrow wooden stairs, then through the workroom to the door that opened on to the back alley. Who did he think he was, bellowing outside her window in the dead of night, and, come to think of it, why was she letting him in?

The last question stopped her with her hand frozen on the deadbolt.

'Emily?' It wasn't a shout, but it was loud enough.

She snapped the bolt back and jerked open the door. He was standing directly on the other side, still wearing that foolish grin, his fingers jammed into the pockets of his jeans, rounding his shoulders under the same black tank-top he'd been wearing that morning. 'Be quiet and get in here!' she whispered viciously.

'Why, thank you kindly, Emily,' he said, walking past her into the dark workroom. 'Nice of you to ask.'

She locked the door behind him and, without a second glance in his direction, stomped back towards the stairs. 'You want coffee?' she shot irritably over her shoulder. 'Fine. I'll make coffee. It's obvious that you could use some.'

She heard his unsteady step behind her as she mounted the stairs, and then his mumbled, 'S'dark in here. Light a candle, for God's sake.'

She flipped the light switch at the top of the stairs, then spun round and glared down at him, hands on hips.

'Wow!' he gasped involuntarily, staring up at her with his blue eyes impossibly wide. He nearly fell down the stairs backwards as he grasped for the railing. 'You can see clear through that damn thing.'

Emily's face went white as she realised what backlighting would do to the thin cotton robe and nightie. She swallowed once, then darted away from his line of sight, into the bedroom, leaving him to find his way for himself. In a panic that was totally unlike her, she shed her nightclothes and scrambled into the first clothes she laid her hands on—the old jeans and baggy white shirt she wore on cleaning days.

He was slumped on her couch when she came out, looking straight at her across the room, smiling.

'I liked the other outfit better,' he said carefully, enunciating each word with exaggerated precision. His hair was tousled in a blond tangle over his forehead, and his eyes were at half-mast, but something she saw in them made Emily wonder—just for a moment—if he was really as drunk as he pretended to be. When he blinked—not really a blink at all; more like a sagging of his eyelids—she dismissed the suspicion instantly. He was drunk, all right. Irresponsibly, irrefutably drunk.

'I'll make the coffee,' she said sharply, turning away from him with a look of disgust.

She stayed in the kitchen the whole ten minutes it took for the coffee-maker to finish, half hoping that he'd have passed out when she emerged, so she wouldn't have to talk to him.

Oh, hell, what are you wishing for? she asked herself suddenly, clapping a hand to her mouth. Wouldn't that look just dandy, Nicholas Simon spending the night? Passed out or not, you know perfectly well what the people in this town would think if they found out.

Now frantic that what she had wished for might come true, she hurried to fill two mugs and bumped the swinging door between the kitchen and living-room with her hip.

'Oh.' She stopped dead on the other side. He was still slouched on the couch—actually, it looked more like he'd been *propped* there—but, for all his limp helplessness, he had apparently managed to walk to the wall switch, turn off the overhead light, and switch on a small table-lamp instead. It cast a warm golden circle on just the right side of his head, but the rest of the room was in shadow.

'Oh,' he mimicked, white teeth flashing. 'Oh, what? Did you think I'd have gone?'

'No,' she said coldly, walking over and stiff-arming the mug towards him. 'I thought you'd have passed out.'

He chuckled deep in his throat, and, with a swiftness that shouldn't have been possible in view of his condition, snatched both mugs from her hands and tipped his head to the space next to him on the couch. 'Sit down, Emily. We'll have a reunion.'

She eyed the space warily, not wanting to sit that close to him, but not wanting him to think he could make her uncomfortable, either. She sat in the opposite corner of the couch, her legs tucked under her, twisted to face him.

He took a noisy slurp from one mug, passed her the other, then flung his left arm across the back of the couch and looked at her. 'There. Isn't this nice? Two old friends, re-newing their relationship. What could be better?'

She eyed his hand warily. It was much too close to her shoulder. 'Almost anything,' she said drily. 'It's two-thirty in the morning, and, in case you've forgotten, we were never friends. We didn't even know each other.'

Nonplussed, he wagged his forefinger at her. 'Ah, but we might have been. As a matter of fact, we might have been a lot more, if you hadn't been so stand-offish in the old days.' His smile seemed to slide across his face. 'I've been wondering for over ten years what you'd be like in bed.'

Emily couldn't help herself. Her mouth fell open and her eyes flew wide.

Nick laughed out loud at her expression. 'Oh, come on, Emily. Don't try to tell me you find the idea offensive.'

'I find everything about you offensive!' she snapped. 'And I always did!'

There was something sly, something absolutely sober about his smile. 'You know what, Emily?' he asked very, very softly. 'I don't believe you. I don't believe you ever found me offensive at all.'

Emily pressed her lips into a tight line and said nothing. There was nothing she could say that would make a dent in conceit like that.

When his gaze and the silence became intolerable, she said, 'Finish your coffee and get out of here.'

He spread his fingers across his chest and affected a wounded expression. 'Just like that? You're going to throw me out in the cold?'

She closed her eyes and turned her head away. 'Just like that.'

When he didn't move after a few seconds, she glanced sideways and found him gazing around the apartment with a bemused expression, completely ignoring her instruction to leave. 'You've got a lot of plants up here,' he murmured, his eyes travelling from the pot-hugging succulents to the towering figs, from the exotic bird-of-paradise to the lowly philodendrons.

'I'm a florist, remember?' she retorted.

He nodded absently.

'Listen, Nick, I don't know why you came here tonight, but it's late, and I want you to leave.'

'You said that before.'

'And I'm going to keep saying it, until you go home.'

He rolled his head to look at her. 'There's nobody there.'

Emily's brows and lips twitched uncertainly, but in the end she refused to let him play on her sympathies. 'So call some of your old schoolfriends. A lot of them still live around here.'

'I didn't want to be with any of them,' he shrugged. 'I wanted to be here, with you.'

'Why?' she demanded.

He shook his head helplessly. 'Damned if I know. I must be out of my mind. But still, it feels right. I like it here.'

'But I don't like *you* here.'

He arched one brow and grinned. 'You will.'

Thoroughly exasperated, she moved to jump up from the couch, but before her feet hit the floor his left hand shot out to close around her upper arm, and he jerked her towards him, pulling her off balance. Caught totally by surprise, she fell sideways on his chest, gasping at the impact. Before she could even digest what had happened, let alone react to it, he had her by the shoulders and had pulled her up until her face was level with his.

'Remember graduation night, Emily?' he said, and his eyes were so close to hers that she couldn't bring them into focus. 'I think it's high time we tried that again, don't you?'

Just as she opened her mouth to fire back a vicious retort, his lips came down hard on hers.

If it hadn't been so unexpected, such an outright shock, she would have exploded away from him in a surge of indignation that would have obliterated all her senses. But for just a fraction of a second she was so stunned by his actions that she froze, just as she had on graduation day, and she was fated to pay dearly for that.

In that brief second of her immobility, the bruising, grinding pressure of his mouth stilled abruptly, almost as if he was as stunned as she was. When his chest hitched beneath her, she became shockingly aware of the blossoming tenderness of her breasts, and the awareness itself horrified her.

'Let *go*,' she tried to say, but the words were lost against his mouth and only the movement of her lips registered. In an immediate response, his hands slid from her shoulders down to her waist, encircling it with a quivering restraint that made her back arch involuntarily.

Even while one part of her mind was recording outrage at what he was doing, another part was recording a volley of unfamiliar stimuli—the strength and breadth of the hands at her waist, the hardness of his mouth, the sandpaper rasp of his jaw against the delicate skin of her face. When she felt her body automatically respond with an accelerated pulse and a strange tingling sensation that began in her breasts and spread quickly downwards, she twisted her mouth from his and gasped, 'Stop!' flattening her hands against his chest, pushing away. With barely a pause, his hands jerked on her back, pulling her against him again. He shuddered visibly when her breasts flattened against him, then blinked in surprise when she pushed away again, her hands curled into fists this time.

'What are you doing, Em?' he breathed, somehow managing to sound innocent in spite of the hoarseness of his voice.

'What are *you* doing?' she countered sharply, trying to twist away. Just when she thought she was close to managing it, his hands shot around to grab her wrists and tug them against his chest.

'You know damn well what I'm doing. The same thing you are. What we should have done ten years ago.'

'No!' She was struggling in earnest now, her face contorted with the effort, and there was one terrifying moment when she was completely aware of his massive size, of his strength, and all that that implied. 'You're drunk!' she cried out, as if that were some sort of magic talisman that would stop him.

All it did was make him laugh. 'That's right. I'm drunk. I can't be held responsible. What's your excuse?' His hands were on her back again, pulling her so sharply against him that the air left her lungs in a rush, but he'd made a mistake. He'd let her hands go, and the right one swung back in an instinctive defence, then crashed into his cheek with a resounding slap.

His arms fell from her back instantly, and for a moment his expression was dumbfounded. While Emily watched wide-eyed, holding her breath, afraid to move now that she finally could, he reached up with one hand and rubbed his cheek. It made a rasping sound against his whiskers that seemed somehow deafening in the quiet apartment.

Slowly, warily, her eyes never leaving his, Emily reached back with her left hand, grabbed the couch cushion behind her, and pulled away. His head turned to follow her progress like a snake matching every movement of its prey, and at the last moment, just as she jumped to her feet, he snatched out at her.

He really was drunk, she realised then, because his reflexes were slow. He only managed to catch the hem of her blouse in his fingers, but a row of buttons strained and popped and flew across the room under the force of his tug. Emily was left standing over him, looking down with horrified dismay at where her blouse hung open, snagged over one shoulder, nearly baring her right breast. She snatched the blouse from his unprotesting fingers and turned her back to cover herself.

'You bastard!' she managed to choke out furiously, spitting the words over her shoulder. 'I want you out of here. I want you out of here right now! I don't care where you go, or how you get there, *but I want you out*!'

She spun back to face him on the last word, her face screwed into a red mask of humiliated fury... and then she caught her breath, blinked in disbelief, and finally remembered to close her sagging jaw.

Nicholas had finally passed out.

CHAPTER THREE

EMILY lay rigidly on her back in bed, her eyes squeezed shut, alert for any sound from the living-room for fear that Nick would...what? Wake up and storm into her bedroom and attack her? If she'd been so worried about something like that, why had she let him in in the first place? Why had she sat right next to him? Why had she waited so long to slap him?

She slammed the door on her thoughts, unable to face them for the moment.

It had been absolutely impossible to waken him. She'd whispered, then demanded, then almost shouted that he wake up, and when that hadn't worked she'd prodded gingerly at his shoulder with one finger, ready to leap backwards in an instant. Finally, totally frustrated, she'd sagged into a chair facing the couch, her chin propped miserably in her hands as she watched him sleep. She didn't dare call anyone to take him home; how would she explain his being there at three o'clock in the morning, and who would she call anyway?

'Bastard,' she'd hissed again at the sleeping figure, but there had been no venom in her tone. He hadn't looked like a bastard, slumped in one corner of the couch, blond hair tumbling over his brow, the strong lines of his face softened in sleep. He'd looked strangely defenceless, vulnerable in spite of his size, and it was when she felt that first peculiar tug at her heart that she'd jumped up from the chair and stormed into her bedroom, hoping he'd wake up miserable and aching and cramped.

Maybe you should have covered him with something, she thought now as she lay in bed. It isn't *that* warm, with the windows wide open, and that tank-top of his is so thin that you can almost see right through it to his chest . . .

She groaned aloud and rolled over and buried her head in the pillow. Everything would be better in the morning. It had to be. Who knew? She might get lucky. Maybe he was so drunk that he wouldn't remember what had happened here tonight; that she had actually—just for a second, mind you—kissed him *back*. Maybe, it there was any justice in the world, he'd remember the slap and forget the kiss, and she'd never have to face that smug grin of his, look into his eyes and see that knowing, mocking look . . .

Her pillow absorbed a long sigh of despair. And maybe there would be an earthquake during the night, and the whole town would be swallowed up in a deep pit. There seemed to be as much chance of one thing happening as the other.

Nick had gone when she woke up and peered out into the living-room, and only a slight indentation on the couch cushions convinced her that he had ever been there at all.

He got up and left before sunrise, she told herself hopefully as she stepped into the shower, and no one will ever find out he was here. He certainly wouldn't advertise it—what reputed ladies' man wanted it known that he was rebuffed by the resident old maid? She lathered her short hair, frowning when she remembered that Nick had called her cut masculine.

The early morning air wafting through the window was brutally dry, promising another blistering day. As sick as she was of the standard garb of shorts, she pulled a fresh white pair from a drawer and stepped into them, then tugged on a clean white tank-top. As she stood in front of the dresser mirror, brushing her damp hair back from her face, her eyes wandered to the generous swell of her breasts beneath the cotton material. The brush stopped in mid-stroke and she blushed.

She'd never paid much attention to her body since that first fearful wonder of puberty; she'd certainly never given a second thought to forgoing a bra in heat like this, not with the green overall concealing her shape so thoroughly. But, overall or not, this morning was different—*she* was different—more aware of her body than she had been in . . . ten years.

With an irritated sigh, she turned away from the mirror and rummaged in her drawer for a bra.

Less than half an hour later she was downstairs, glass cleaner in one hand, cloth in the other, busily polishing every flat surface in the showroom.

She always opened the shop a full hour before most people had finished their breakfast, using the quiet time to perform the daily cleaning that had become ritual. A place for everything, everything in its place, and, above all, everything gleaming.

The long formica counter-top had always been her nemesis, so worn from years of service that the lustre was gone. Still she polished it diligently every day, trying to buff back to life a shine that had died years before. She was standing in front of the counter, her back to the door, rubbing vigorously when the bell jingled the arrival of her first customer.

'Good morning, Em.'

She shot upright at his deep voice, then forced herself to bend back to her work without looking around. The heat of colour rose to her face, and she tried to will it away. He was even more arrogant than she'd thought, coming here on the heels of last night's fiasco. Unless he'd come to apologise, of course. She considered the possibility for a fraction of a second, then dismissed it. More likely he'd come to gloat. If he remembered anything at all.

'Don't tell me you're going to ignore a man who just spent the night with you, Emily.'

The cloth in her right hand moved in faster, smaller circles and she gritted her teeth.

As he came up to stand at her left, the first thing she was aware of was the faint scent of soap, and then, beneath that, a more elusive fragrance. It's his scent, she thought, frowning down at the formica. What you're smelling is the very distinctive scent of one particular man, identifying it as one animal identifies another. That she was capable of such a thing astonished her, horrified her, and she rubbed even harder, her lower lip caught between her teeth.

'You work too hard, Emily.'

She flinched when he leaned on the counter, his hands laced together, his right forearm right next to her left. Out of the corner of her eye she could see that he was staring at the back wall, not even looking at her. She inched away until there was a wide space between their arms. Without commenting, almost absently, he mimicked her move until his forearm was pressed against hers again.

This is stupid, she told herself, trying to rub the pattern right off the speckled white formica, pretending not to notice him. He can chase me right off the edge of the counter if we keep this up.

Suddenly the fingers of his left hand were on her arm, and the circular motion of the cloth stopped dead.

'Look, Em,' he murmured, and reluctantly, knowing it was a mistake, she risked a quick glance at his profile.

He was wearing a white short-sleeved shirt, open to expose a tanned throat, and he looked impossibly cool and crisp, as if heat never affected him. His head was bent, shiny blond wisps dangling from his forehead, and he was staring raptly at their two forearms, lying side by side. She followed his gaze.

'It's amazing, isn't it?' he went on in a deep, soft, hypnotic murmur. With every word he spoke, his breath puffed against the skin of her arm, snapping the tiny, almost invisible blonde hairs there to attention. 'The difference between man and woman, so obvious, so simple on the surface, and yet so profound.' His fingers trailed delicately from her inner elbow down to her wrist, making the hair on the back of her neck stand up. She told her arm to jerk away, but it just lay there, obstinately refusing to obey.

'Look at it, Em. Look at the difference.'

The command was entirely unnecessary. She was so mesmerised by his voice, so helplessly caught up in what he was saying, that she had forgotten to breathe. She stared down at where his broad, muscular forearm pressed against her much slimmer one; where his wide wrist mocked the delicate bones of her own;

where the power of his splayed hand sug-
gested that hers could be crushed in its grip.
Her skin tingled where his crisp blond hairs
brushed against it, and she exhaled quietly.

'It's a good difference, Emily. A natural
one. It's nothing to be afraid of.'

'I'm not afraid.'

'Oh, yes, you are,' he murmured, still
looking down at their arms lying side by side.
'You were afraid the first time I kissed you
ten years ago, and you were afraid again last
night.'

She caught her breath silently and held it.

'Are you afraid every time a man kisses
you, Emily? Or just me?'

'I'm not afraid!' The words tumbled out in
a rush as she jerked her arm off the counter
and backed away from him. He turned towards her, showing the left side of his face for
the first time. 'Oh, lord!' she whispered.

It wasn't much of a black eye, as far as
black eyes went. As a matter of fact, the red
and purple discoloration didn't surround the
eye at all. It was off to one side, towards the

temple, barely touching the outside corner. Still, it was brilliantly visible, and to Emily it looked like an accusing finger, pointed directly at her.

'Did I do that?' she asked in a small voice.

He smiled briefly. 'You've got a mean right hook, Emily, but not that mean. This wound,' he reached up to touch the spot, wincing, 'was self-inflicted. It was dark when I left this morning. I walked into a wall on my way out.'

Her relief was so great that she allowed herself a little smile—not only because she wasn't responsible for his injury, but also because he'd left her apartment when it was still dark. No one ever had to know.

As if her smile had been an invitation, he reached over to brush her cheek with the backs of his curled fingers.

She scowled and backed away from his hand.

He took a step towards her, touched her cheek again. This time she reached up and plucked his hand away from her face. 'Stop that.'

One of his brows quirked. 'You didn't seem to mind when I touched you last night. Not until you remembered you were supposed to.'

His hand went right back up to her cheek, and she slapped it down angrily. 'You were drunk last night!' she retorted, as if his drunkenness somehow explained her behaviour.

He laughed out loud at the twisted reasoning, then jammed his fingers into the front pockets of his jeans and looked down at the tops of his tennis shoes. 'Yes, Emily. I certainly was. About as drunk as I've ever been in my life.'

She wrinkled her nose primly, folded her arms across her chest, and waited for a long moment. 'Well,' she said finally, 'aren't you going to apologise?'

He turned his head slowly and met her eyes head-on, and for some reason Emily felt as if she'd been punched in the stomach. 'The only thing I'll apologise for is passing out. Everything else was forgivable. That wasn't. And it won't happen again.'

Her laugh was supposed to sound dis-
dainful, but it came out a little weak. 'It most
certainly won't, because that's the last time
you'll ever see the inside of my apartment...'
she began, but then he tipped his head back,
just a little, and looked down at her through
narrowed lids, his eyes suddenly a darker blue.
She didn't quite understand why the rest of
her sentence trailed away into nothingness—
maybe it had something to do with the way
he was looking at her...almost as if he wasn't
looking *at* her at all, but into some secret place
inside that even she hadn't known existed. It
was a compelling gaze, a commanding one,
and the sheer force of it took her by surprise.

'I didn't expect it, either,' he murmured,
barely moving his lips, his gaze so brilliantly
fixed on hers that it felt like a physical connection. 'But last night was just the beginning, Emily. It isn't going to end there. My
goodness, your eyes are green, the colour of
spring.'

She blinked once, frozen by his expression,
her thoughts short-circuiting crazily. No, she

remembered suddenly; that's not right. Algae. That's the colour of my eyes. Like the algae on Martin's livestock pond.

Somehow the everyday nature of that thought slashed through her dreamlike state and brought her sharply to her senses. He was seducing her. And she was just standing there, letting it happen.

A muscle twitched its warning just beneath her right eye, but apparently Nick hadn't noticed.

'You're beautiful, you know.' He took both her hands and brought them up to his chest. 'And tonight you're going to feel beautiful. I promise.'

She focused on the corner of his mouth that was curved upwards, wondering why she'd never noticed that slight indentation there, just to the left of his lips. He must smile like that often, she thought, with just one side of his mouth. That was the mark of a cynic, wasn't it? A person perpetually amused by the gullibility of others?

'Really?' she said, her voice suddenly flat and cold.

'Really. You'll see. Trust me, Em.'

His pretence at earnestness would have been comical, if his motives hadn't been so obvious, so juvenile, so despicable. She jerked her hands down, out of his grasp, back to her sides, and the suddenness of the gesture startled him. He actually seemed to recoil from whatever it was he saw in her face, and Emily liked that.

'You tell me I'm beautiful and I hop into bed, is that how it goes?' she asked sarcastically. She felt ten feet tall, infinitely superior, magnificently haughty.

Unfortunately, after that one second of startled confusion, he actually seemed amused by her posturing. The tiny lines around his eyes had deepened, and he was wearing that stupid, one-sided grin of his. 'Something like that,' he replied steadily.

She clenched her jaw and glared at him.

His smile broadened a little. 'You will, you know. Eventually, you will, Emily. I can wait.'

She pulled in a huge breath that would have fuelled a thousand words, then closed her lips on it when the bell over the shop door jingled.

'Hello, Emily dear.'

Oh, lord. Mrs Hoeffer. Ancient, lilac-scented, blue-haired Mrs Hoeffer, in for the Tuesday bouquet for her bridge luncheon. As dear a soul as lived in this town, and as garrulous a soul as lived in the whole damn state.

Emily jerked her head like a marionette wearing a painted smile. 'Good morning, Mrs Hoeffer. How are you? Lovely day, isn't it? I have your flowers all ready for you in the cooler. You know Nick Simon, don't you? Art's grandson? Why don't you two have a little chat while I get your order? It'll take just a minute.'

She dashed back into the workroom, straight to the tiny mirror, and peered worriedly at her face. Except it wasn't her face. It belonged to some other woman. Some stupid, flustered woman with unnaturally bright eyes and terribly flushed cheeks... flushed? They were downright scarlet.

She blew air out through her cheeks, took several deep, calming breaths, then looked warily into the mirror again. There. That was a little better; a little less colourful, anyway. She held the cooler door open longer than necessary, letting the chill air finish what the deep breathing had started, then she breezed back into the showroom with a bright smile that sagged when there was no one to see it.

Nick and Mrs Hoeffer were huddled by the front window, his arm over her plump shoulders while she giggled like a schoolgirl.

'Oh, *Nicky*!' she tittered, slapping his hand playfully. 'You haven't changed a bit!'

You can say that again, Emily thought bitterly. He's still incorrigible. With a vicious jab, she punched the total button on the cash register and the little bell rang.

'Oh! Emily, dear!' Mrs Hoeffer turned around, and Emily would have bet her life that the woman hadn't blushed like that in sixty years. He'd probably propositioned her, too. 'Back so soon? I've just been having the nicest talk with Nicky here...' Suddenly she looked from one to the other, almost mischievously, then she covered her mouth and giggled again. 'I really must be going now.'

Emily smiled uncertainly as Mrs Hoeffer bustled to the counter, paid for the bouquet, snatched her cone-shaped package and hurried towards the door. At the last moment she turned around and smiled one of those smiles old people bestowed on favoured grandchildren. 'I'm very, very happy for you, Emily dear,' she said, 'and I won't tell a *soul* about the black eye, I promise!' Then she bounced out of the door, fairly bursting with whatever information she had just promised not to tell. She waggled her fingers merrily as she passed the big front window on her way down the street.

Slowly, slowly, Emily's head turned towards Nick, her eyes narrowed in suspicion. He was leaning back against the door-frame, grinning at her, his legs crossed at the ankles, his arms folded across his chest.

'What was she talking about?'

He shrugged innocently.

'*What*?' she repeated, green eyes flashing.

He pushed away from the door and walked back to lean towards her over the counter.

'Did you know Mrs Hoeffer used to bake cookies for me?'

'No, I didn't know Mrs Hoeffer used to bake cookies for you,' she repeated impatiently. 'So what's that got to do with anything?'

'Well, every week she'd bake three dozen cookies and make her husband drive her out to the farm so she could deliver them. Guess she thought I'd die of a cookie shortage or something, living out there alone with Grandpa.'

'Fascinating. Is this story going anywhere?'

He shook his head, disappointed. 'Every story goes somewhere, Emily. They're all worth hearing, you know.'

She sighed, exasperated, but he pretended not to notice.

'This story, for instance, establishes background. Mrs Hoeffer and I are old friends, and in the way of old friends we were just catching up on the news. I asked her if the bursitis in her shoulder was responding to medication——'

Emily frowned. 'Mrs Hoeffer has bursitis?'

'And she asked me where I got this.' He grinned and pointed to the bruise. 'I told her you slapped me.'

'*What?*' she breathed, grabbing the edge of the counter so hard that all the colour bled from her fingertips. 'You told her *I* did that?'

'Of course not. That would have been a lie.'

'But you just said——'

'I said that she asked where I got the bruise, and, in a totally unrelated thought, I chose that particular moment to make mention of the fact that you slapped me. That's all.'

'That's *all*?' she shouted. 'But you *know* what she'll think! And if you really know Mrs Hoeffer, you also know that within the next thirty minutes everyone in town will be thinking exactly the same thing!' She slammed her mouth closed furiously. Of course he knew. Look at that grin. Look at those eyes. 'Fine!' she snapped viciously. 'You want the whole town to think I decked you? Well, that's just fine with me. Should put a well-deserved crack in that old Casanova reputation of yours, and, in addition to that, it makes my position abundantly clear!'

'Maybe,' he said lazily. 'Then again, maybe not. You see, I explained that it was a late-night lovers' quarrel in your apartment, just before we went to bed.'

'Oh, hell,' she mouthed, face falling.

'Well, it was the truth, right? It did happen in your apartment, it was late at night, and afterwards we both went to bed. You certainly can't blame me if Mrs Hoeffer reads more into it than what I said.'

Emily didn't know whether to scream or cry, so she just stood there, mute, while the options played havoc with her expression. Nick's smile was gentle, almost sympathetic.

'Well, I've got some things that need doing this morning.' He pushed away from the counter and lifted his arms over his head in a mighty stretch. A casual, indifferent stretch, as if he'd done absolutely nothing wrong. 'I'll be back at about noon to take you to lunch. Is Alfred's Café as good as it used to be?'

For a moment, Emily's voice was lost in the open cavern of her mouth. Finally she managed to croak, 'Why are you doing this?'

He cocked his head a bit, almost as if the question surprised him. 'You're a big girl, Emily. You figure it out.'

She ground her teeth together so hard that it hurt.

'Look at it this way.' He grinned devilishly. 'Your standing in the community will sky-rocket, once they've all heard you're sleeping with me.'

Emily gaped, hardly able to believe that one man could support an ego of that size, even while she was listening to the evidence of it.

Nick just chuckled and walked to the door, then turned back towards her in an after-thought. 'It's really too hot for a bra, Emily, don't you think?' he asked casually.

And then, while her mouth and her eyes were still forming three enormous circles, he went out of the door.

CHAPTER FOUR

NOT a single customer passed through the shop door before noon, and still it was the most harrowing morning of Emily's life. She spent most of the time wandering aimlessly through the displays, touching a leaf here, a flower there, as if she could find some sort of reassurance in the static plant life; some sort of guarantee that the world was still right-side-up and the past twenty-four hours had only been a bad dream.

Why was he doing this to her? Why would he deliberately set out to compromise her reputation? Simply because she'd slapped him?

'You're a big girl, Emily. You figure it out.' His words echoed like a challenge in her mind.

At mid-morning she glanced at the clock and thought that, if Mrs Hoeffer was up to her usual standard, by this time everyone in town would believe that she was sleeping with

Nick Simon. Good lord. If it weren't so embarrassing, so maddening, it would be almost laughable. Sleeping with someone? She'd barely been kissed in all of her twenty-seven years, and, almost without exception, those men who had risked it had slunk away nursing a bruised ego.

Except Nick, of course, proud owner of the most inflated ego of all. So inflated, in fact, that when he'd finally been rejected last night—probably for the first time in his life—he'd absolutely refused to accept it . . .

Her thoughts slammed to a halt. Of course. Of *course*. All this time she'd been looking for some deep, profound motive in a man who probably hadn't had a deep, profound thought in his life. Her slap hadn't hurt him, but her rejection had been an unacceptable affront. He might have left Random years ago, but you didn't leave behind the standards a place like this seared into your mind—standards that dictated that men commanded, and women obeyed. She had had the audacity to ignore that basic principle, and Nick was out to teach her a lesson.

Once she'd figured it out, she could hardly wait for his return, for another shot at putting him in his place. If Nick Simon wanted to play power games, he'd chosen the wrong adversary.

He was back at the shop just as the noon siren set every dog in town howling. He sauntered in with the slick confidence of a man who had never confronted an indifferent woman, and inside, at least, Emily smiled to see it. The bigger they are...she thought smugly.

It was a little disconcerting when he totally ignored her carefully rehearsed, barbed refusal to have even another conversation with him, let alone a public lunch. It was more disconcerting when he followed her out on to the street, actually grabbing at her arm, laughing at her futile attempts to shake him off. She turned on him then, actually shouting, slapping at his hands when they reached for her, finally concluding in a furious, red-faced bellow that she wouldn't have lunch with him if he were the last man on earth with a sandwich and she were starving to death.

She'd known, of course, that every ear on Main Street was attuned to the confrontation—public quarrels were a novel occurrence in the quiet little town—but that didn't bother her. Let them all hear how she really felt about him, and Mrs Hoeffer's tale would die a rapid, painless death.

But somehow it didn't work that way. When her tirade finally ended, she looked smugly at the faces watching from up and down the block, and suddenly felt as if she were in a bad performance of *The Taming of the Shrew*. They were all smiling. Every one. Dammit, they were almost beaming.

So it was that by suppertime that night every soul in Random knew that quiet, conservative, some might even say prim Emily Swenson was having a tempestuous love-affair with that charming Nicky Simon. So tempestuous, in fact, that they'd had an ear-splitting shouting match right on Main Street at high noon, in front of God and everybody. Who would have guessed, they whispered among themselves, that the heat of such passion had been buried in their own stiff-necked Emily all these years, just waiting for the right man to bring it to a boil?

No one said that directly to her, of course, but she had a steady stream of suspicious customers that afternoon, people who'd never bought a flower in their lives. 'Just browsing,' they said, sauntering around the shop with guilty little smiles, sneaking peeks at her as if she were some exotic animal they'd just found living in their midst.

That night Emily locked her door and slammed her windows and pulled all the shades, then waited, trembling, for Nick Simon to start caterwauling under her bedroom window again. He'd sworn to do just that if she continued to rebuff him, and she was ready, a full bucket of ice water stationed right next to the window.

By midnight the ice had melted, the water was tepid, and Emily felt as if she'd been run through the wringers of an old washing-machine three or four times. Defeated, exhausted from hours of tension, she went to bed in the stifling heat of the closed apartment—still wearing her bra.

There was a long bright red convertible parked directly in front of the shop when she opened for business the next morning. It had blazing white leather seats and a frivolous, feathery thing attached to the radio aerial. It was an insolent-looking car, too bright, too garish for the drab, dusty Main Street of drought-plagued Random—precisely the kind of car she'd expect Nicholas Simon to own.

She took one timid step out on to the pavement, peering this way and that to make sure she wasn't observed trying to get a closer look.

Main Street was as still as the early morning heat hanging over the town. The pavements were empty, the store-fronts dark, the street deserted. If they'd had a traffic light in town, she would have been able to hear it blinking. She took two more steps towards the car.

'Morning!' He popped out of the doorway of the hardware store next door, startling her so badly that she had to stifle a scream.

For a moment, she couldn't find her voice. The hand that had flown automatically to her chest recorded the frightened pounding of her heart through her green florist's coat, the sleeveless blouse, and the bra underneath.

'Sorry,' he grinned sheepishly, stepping out to the middle of the pavement. 'I didn't mean to scare you.'

'I'll bet,' she said acidly, then fixed him with a cold glare. He was wearing a light blue T-shirt that matched his eyes, with short sleeves straining over the smooth rise of tanned biceps. At least it was a more decent covering than the tank-top he'd worn on that first day, but, as if to counter the extra material on top, he'd traded his jeans for a pair of abbreviated white running shorts. Her eyes dropped involuntarily to long, ridged thighs and the angular musculature of a runner's calves.

'You like my legs?' he asked happily, following her gaze, turning on the toes of his tennis shoes in a comical preen.

'Oh, stop it!' she hissed, jerking her eyes up to the relatively harmless sweep of blond over his brow, then back to the car. 'This thing is yours, I take it?'

He strolled over to the car, patted the bonnet affectionately, then leaned back against it with his arms braced to either side. The thin cloth of his shirt clung to stomach muscles that rippled with the gesture. 'This "thing" happens to be a '66 Chevy Malibu — a classic. Pretty, isn't she?'

Emily scowled at the chauvinistic propensity to ascribe the female gender to possessions. '*She* is taking up two parking spaces,' she said frigidly.

'Now, now.' He moved to push away from the car, but when she scrambled back two panicked steps he froze, then leaned back again. 'Oh-oh. You're angry, aren't you? I was afraid you might be, when I didn't show up last night after I promised, but I just couldn't get away from——'

'Move the car.'

He was silent for a beat. 'Move the car?'

'Move the car,' she repeated.

Sunlight bounced off his head when he shook it. 'Can't.'

'What do you mean, you can't? Why?'

'Well, the truth is it's awfully dusty out at the farm. All those dirt roads, and all those ploughed fields drying up, you know. There's no garage, and the barn is just stuffed with old machinery. No room for the Chevy in there. So I decided I'd just leave my car in town and use Grandpa's old truck to get around instead.'

'You think you're going to just *leave* this here, right in front of my shop?'

'Seemed like a good place to me,' he shrugged innocently.

'It's *not* a good place! It's an *awful* place! You leave this car here all the time and everyone's going to think...'

He smiled at her, waiting patiently for her to finish.

'I'll call the sheriff,' she finally threatened, her face red.

'Well, you can do that, of course, but I already asked him if there was any law against leaving the car parked outside your place all night, and you know what he said? Nothing. He didn't say a thing. Just winked at me.'

Emily clenched her jaw against the whirlpool of helpless rage threatening to explode inside her head. 'Leave me alone!' she finally shouted.

She spun on her heel and stormed back into the shop, but he was right behind her. As she reached the counter he grabbed her left wrist and jerked her around and against him with hardly any effort at all.

'You don't want me to leave you alone, Emily.'

Just as he started to bend his head towards hers, her free arm flew up and back and started a power swing towards his face. In a blur of motion his hand shot up and grabbed her wrist, then he slammed both her arms down and held them pressed against her sides. As she glared up at him, her face twisted with the frustrated effort to free herself, she saw a dark, controlled anger tighten his features, and caught her breath. He didn't even look like Nick Simon any more. There was no happy indifference in that rigid expression; no happy-go-lucky charm.

'Once, Emily,' he warned her. 'I let you get away with that once, but that's your limit. Don't raise your hand to me again.'

It was partly the change seriousness wrought in his face that made her gape with amazement, and it was partly uncertainty. She knew how to deal with a cocksure, insolent Nick Simon; she had no idea how to manage the man who stood before her now.

Like a mindless automaton, she let herself be backed against the counter, her wrists still pinned at her sides, the position of her arms throwing her chest out. She felt her hands open and her fingers press against the rough wood base as he walked into her, bent his head, then froze for a moment, his mouth a fraction of an inch from hers. He held her with his eyes and his hands while the full length of his body—were men's bodies all so hard?—pushed tight against hers, forcing a soft gasp from her throat. His breath was warm, then hot as it broke against her chin, and a few strands of his hair brushed across her eyebrow like tiny filaments charged with electricity.

'Do you always have to force yourself on women?' she managed to hiss at him.

'This is force?' he asked wryly, and then, as if to counter the brute strength with which he held her, his lips plucked delicately at hers, so soft, so warmly gentle, that for a moment she forgot she was at war. It seemed almost innocent, this kissing—just a harmless, wonderfully natural thing that flooded your senses with such a sense of well-being that there couldn't possibly be anything wrong with it.

Helplessly, Emily's lips softened and moved in a response that was pure instinct, since she had no experience to engineer it.

He pulled away a fraction of an inch, just enough to move his lips in a whisper that she felt more than she heard. 'And this?' His tongue swept over her lips and she went rigid. 'Is this force, too?' His tongue found the corner of her mouth, ran along the inside of her upper lip to the other corner, and then, heaven help her, she shuddered against him, her body saying things her mind would never permit her to utter.

Feeling it, apparently stunned by it, Nick sucked in a quick, hard gasp that was an explosion of sound in the quiet shop, and then everything suddenly shifted into high speed.

His mouth moved desperately, hungrily, tongue probing between the seam of her lips, his breathing as hard and fast as the heart she felt beating against her breast. Was it hers? Or his? For an instant, all the mysteries of the universe seemed to hinge on that particular riddle, but her mind refused to address it. It was far too busy concentrating on the more urgent problem of simply remembering how to breathe.

At last Nick pulled his lips from hers to draw air in through his mouth, letting his forehead rest momentarily against hers. 'Hot,' he breathed, his eyes closed. 'So damn hot. I knew it. Everyone else thought I was crazy, but even ten years ago I knew I could do this to you.'

She went suddenly stiff, pressing the small of her back against the counter. She jerked her head to one side. 'Do *what* to me?' She made her voice cold. 'Pin me down and force yourself on me? A gorilla could do that much.'

The words sounded wonderful, even her tone was the perfect combination of revulsion and disdain; the problem was that, even as she was speaking them, there was this peculiar red-hot pool of feeling deep in the pit of her stomach which she couldn't seem to turn off. In some way it seemed connected to his hands on her wrist, the pressure of his body against hers. If he would just move away, surely it would go with him?

As if he'd heard her thoughts, he backed away a step and released her wrists, holding his palms up with a dark, confident smile— look, Ma, no hands. Emily caught her lower lip between her teeth. The feeling was still there. Maybe it was connected to his eyes, too. She started to move away, but his hands dropped to the counter on either side of her, trapping her. 'I might have forced you to stand still, Emily,' he said smoothly, 'but I didn't force anything else. You wanted it as much as I did.'

She swallowed once, pressed her lips together in determination, then ducked beneath his arms and skittered away to put the counter between them. Once safely on the other side, she raised her eyes defiantly.

He hadn't moved. He was still standing with his arms braced on the counter, blue eyes intense with a heat that flared deep beneath the surface expression of amusement. 'Come here, Emily,' he said quietly, but for some reason she had the impression that he had shouted.

She stood there without moving, her fingers pressing hard against the sides of her thighs. 'Come here.' He said it again, and the words coursed through her body like an electric current, and finally, with something like horror, she realised that she wanted to obey. Oh, lord—to *obey*.

The connection between them snapped in that instant, and she let her eyes fall closed briefly as she released a long sigh of relief. She was free again.

'What are you doing, Emily?' he asked quietly, not moving, sensing that something had changed.

'I'm not "doing" anything, Nick. I already did it. I walked away from you, just as I did on graduation night, just as I did in my apartment, just as I'll continue to do every time you touch me.'

The indentation between his brows deepened, and Emily felt a cold surge of satisfaction. At least she'd managed to wipe that cocky grin off his face. But not for long. It reappeared almost instantly.

'Have you noticed, Emily, that it takes you a little longer each time? And eventually you're not going to be able to walk away at all.'

'Don't bet on it,' she said icily, and his brows crashed down over the blue chips of his eyes.

'Is that a challenge?'

Emily's smile was placid, chilling. 'That's a promise, and don't take it so personally, Nick. I'm just not interested.'

His eyes narrowed and a muscle in his jaw clamped down hard. 'The hell you aren't.'

She raised her brows and made herself shrug, the picture of nonchalance.

His long arm flashed over the counter before she realised what was happening, and his fingers pressed white circles into the flesh of her forearm. 'The hell you aren't,' he repeated in a menacing tone, but there was the first trace of uncertainty in it as well, and absolutely no humour.

Their eyes locked in a silent battle of wills, and she was holding her own brilliantly, glaring at him with just the right measure of contempt, when his thumb began to move on her arm. She held his gaze, kept her expression stiff, but even she could feel something flash in her eyes—something hot and vibrant that she hadn't wanted him to see. His gaze had been fixed on her face, watching for something, alert for every nuance of her expression. When she'd felt that single, uncontrollable flash, his face had relaxed instantly, his mouth had curled in a satisfied smile, and he'd released her arm. Within the space of a second, he was the old, disturbingly confident Nick again.

Emily's brows twitched, and she caught herself just before it turned into a full-fledged frown of uncertainty. 'I'd like you to leave now.'

He laughed out loud, propped his elbows on the counter and dropped his chin into his hands, gazing at her with a lazy, sceptical smile. 'I'll just bet you would, Emily. Did I tell you I loved your hair?'

She dropped her head and brushed furiously at the front of her green florist's coat.

'Do that again,' he murmured, and she looked up to find him gazing boldly at her bustline.

She spun until her back was to him, her fists knotted, her nostrils flaring.

'You have a striking face, you know.' His voice floated over her shoulder. 'Those high cheekbones, that marvellous brow...long hair would be an insult to a face like that. A distraction.'

'I'm letting it grow!' she snapped with childish spite.

'I'll just cut it off again when you're sleeping, some night when you're so exhausted from lovemaking that you won't even wake up.'

Emily swallowed and felt a shudder pass through her body.

'What are you really afraid of, Em?' he asked softly from behind her.

She let her eyes fall closed in despair, then took a short, hitching breath and turned to face him. 'I'm not afraid of anything,' she said calmly. 'I told you, I'm just not interested.'

He dropped his hands to the counter and looked right at her. 'It's going to be a fight to the finish with you, isn't it?' There was a little smile playing at the corners of his mouth. 'But you know what? It's going to be worth it. In the end, when we finally go to bed together, it's going to be absolutely spectacular.'

CHAPTER FIVE

BEGINNING with the very next day, Nicholas became Emily's shadow, trailing her through the shop, peering over her shoulder with pretended interest in what she was doing, occasionally falling into silence when they were alone, but always making a great show of amiable chatter for the benefit of any customer who came in. He seemed oblivious to her outraged protests, and gradually they lessened in intensity, simply because they were pointless.

'Shouldn't you be getting back to that big city practice of yours?' she finally asked in exasperation after nearly tripping over him.

'Not yet. I'm on leave.'

'What about your patients? What if one of them needs you?'

'I work in a clinic, Emily, with a lot of other doctors. My patients are being very well taken care of. Besides, I needed this time more than they needed me.'

Her face tightened with disapproval. 'A *real* doctor wouldn't desert the people who depend on him.'

He looked at her with a gentle, somewhat surprised smile, as if she had just stated some profound, universal truth he hadn't expected her to grasp. 'You're absolutely right about that, Emily.'

By the second day he'd taken to touching her casually—a hand on her arm in passing, a pat on the head whenever he thought he could get away with it. Shrugging off such harmless physical contact became tedious with repetition, almost ridiculous, and if she were truly as indifferent as she was pretending she'd just ignore it, wouldn't she? So she did. There were a couple of satisfying moments when she caught him watching her with a puzzled frown, no doubt wondering why his campaign of torment wasn't producing the expected reaction. At those times the temptation to smile was strong, but she fought it.

Whatever else Nicholas Simon was, he had a bulldog's persistence. He followed her to the grocery, up and down the aisles and through the check-out; to the hardware store; even on an aimless, silent walk through the town. And yet, as closely as he trailed her during the day, he had never again shown up at her apartment at night. It was such a glaring inconsistency that Emily almost wanted to ask him why, but cold silence was her only defence against him, so she stifled her curiosity.

Of course every resident in Random believed he spent every night with her, thanks to the constant presence of that outlandish car on the street out front. Emily seethed inside whenever she met someone's knowing leer or slyly arched brow, but after a series of flustered denials, each met with much tongue-clucking scepticism, she gave up. She didn't know what lies he was spreading, but apparently they were effective. The townspeople clung to the Nick-and-Emily fabrication like ageing children reluctant to give up a belief in Santa Claus. They *wanted* to believe she was sleeping with Nick Simon. They *wanted* to believe their dead little town was hosting the romance of the century, and finally she said to hell with them all. They'd been duped by a master, and they deserved the shame-faced guilt that would come eventually, when they learned the truth.

On Friday he broke the pattern of his constant presence by popping in and out of the shop, sometimes gone for as long as an hour. Emily struggled to relish the privacy — the first she'd had since he'd begun this ridiculous shadowing crusade — but the odd thing was that she caught herself listening for the bell over the door whenever he left, waiting for his return. Especially this time. It was almost four o'clock, and he'd been gone since two. The silence in the shop was like that pregnant, terrifying silence before a storm, when you huddled in the basement and wondered what form it would take, when it would arrive, and whether or not you would survive it.

'Hi, Em.' Nick's head poked through the door and her feet nearly left the floor.

'Thought I'd let you know I have some things to do. Won't be back for the rest of the day.'

She made a tight little prune-face and ignored him.

'Will you miss me?'

She couldn't resist one sarcastic lash. 'Desperately.'

He grinned, closed the door behind him, then immediately opened it again, just far enough to poke his head around the edge. 'For Pete's sake, Emily, you could fry an egg on the pavement today. Take that silly bra off before you go out to your parents', at least.'

She was deep into a thoroughly satisfying scowl before she thought to wonder how he knew she was having dinner with her parents.

Carl Swenson's farm lay three miles west of town, right off the two-lane tar road that formed Random's Main Street. It wasn't the prettiest land in the area, with barely a tree to interrupt the flow of cropland, but it boasted some of the richest loam on the northern border of America's breadbasket. As desolate as it appeared for most of the year, at harvest time it was spectacularly beautiful—an endless sea of golden wheat and corn-filled plain marching off to the horizon—and the people who knew the land could even see its beauty in spring, when the rich black-brown colour of freshly turned soil promised a future bounty.

But this year was different. The normally plentiful April rains had veered to the south, again and again, and the landscape looked starved and pale. The ploughed and planted fields were dangerously dry, seeds lying dormant and lifeless, topsoil blowing away with the slightest breeze.

The land looked bleached, Emily thought as her car sped westward to her parents' farm. Three more weeks, her father had said; if they didn't get rain by then, the whole year's crop would be lost.

She sighed as she turned the car on to a lane that bisected the drying field on her right. The driveway was typically Midwestern—a long dirt track as straight as the thoughts of a farmer, heading right for the big red barn at the back without so much as a pause at the two-storey white farmhouse. It seemed to say that the barn was the only worthy destination for any visitor, but Emily stopped her car right next to the house and climbed the steps to the back porch.

The oversized, cluttered kitchen was fragrant with the aroma of beef, onions, potatoes and carrots all roasting in a pan together. Her mother looked up from the sink in surprise, her dripping hands suspended over the soapy water.

'Well, hello, dear. I didn't expect you so soon.' She was wearing a peach dress that flattered her complexion and complemented her dark hair, but it was long-sleeved and cinched tightly at the waist, and had to be uncomfortable in this heat.

Emily walked over and kissed her lightly on the cheek. 'I closed the shop early today, Mom. I must have known you were making pot roast. What are you doing in that hot dress on a day like today? You should be in shorts and a halter.'

'Your father loves this dress,' she replied with a smile that spoke of secrets.

Emily shook her head, thinking that her mother would wear feed sacks, if that was what Carl Swenson wanted.

'Grab a cup, dear. We'll have some coffee before it's time to make the salad.' She looked at Emily, her brows raised expectantly. 'So!' she said, grabbing a towel to dry her hands while that 'so' hung in the air. It was the traditional beginning of all the serious talks they'd ever had, a verbal gunshot that warned the listener that her next words, no matter how innocent they seemed, were important. 'That Nicky has certainly grown into a handsome young man, hasn't he?'

Emily could have sworn that the air in the kitchen had suddenly become electrified. 'Nicky?' she asked innocently, easing herself into a chair at the round wooden table.

'Nicky Simon, of course.' Her mother smiled as she sat down.

You old fox, Emily thought, careful to keep her expression blank. You've heard the talk, and, if I know you, you're hoping it's all true. 'When did you see him?'

'Oh, I ran into him somewhere,' her mother replied vaguely, looking around as if she'd never seen her own kitchen before.

'Really? Where?'

Her mother turned her head and looked at Emily, eyes wide with feigned innocence. 'What, dear?'

'I asked where you ran into Nick Simon, Mother.'

'Oh. Well, here, actually.'

'*Here?* Nick was out *here*?'

Her mother shrugged with a guilty little smile.

Emily leaned back in her chair and narrowed her eyes. 'OK, Mom. Let's have it. What on earth was Nick Simon doing out here?'

'He was just paying a call, dear. A *social* call. Being neighbourly, you might say.'

'He's not your neighbour,' Emily pointed out. 'His grandfather's farm is on the other side of town.'

Her mother looked straight into her eyes. 'We're all neighbours in a town this size, Emily. You know that.'

'Baloney,' Emily muttered. It was as profane a word as was ever spoken in this house. 'Nick Simon isn't neighbourly, and he doesn't pay social calls unless he thinks he can get something out of it.'

'Oh?' Mary's brows lifted blithely. 'The way I hear it, he pays quite a few social calls on you, dear.'

Emily scowled, exasperated. 'Forget what you heard, Mother. None of it is true. It's all a lie, all part of some bizarre plan of his—to drive me crazy, I think.' She sighed, thoroughly frustrated, because that had sounded preposterous even to her.

She leaned across the table and spoke earnestly. 'The truth is that he came howling under my window on the night of his grandfather's funeral, drunk as a lord, threatening to wake the town if I didn't let him in. So I did. I let him in, I made him some coffee...then he passed out on the couch. That's *all* that happened. He's just having the time of his life letting the town think there was a whole lot more to it.'

'I see.' Her mother sighed sympathetically, but it was clear that the sympathy was meant for Nick. 'He took Art's death very hard, didn't he? It was nice that he had you to come to for comfort.'

Emily rolled her eyes. 'He wasn't looking for comfort,' she said firmly.

Mary pulled absently at a strand of her hair, but there was a warning in her normally placid green eyes. 'Are you really so sure about that? He was absolutely devoted to his grandfather, you know.'

Emily made a sound of impatience and turned her head.

'He never missed a month; not in ten years,' Mary went on, musing. 'Art was so proud of that. Third weekend of every month, just like clockwork, Nicky would come home. It had to be hard for him, especially during those years when he was working and going to school.'

Emily looked back at her mother, a frown building behind her eyes. 'He came home once a month?' she murmured. 'But I never saw him...'

'He came to visit Art, not the town,' Mary smiled, then she cocked her head, reconsidering what she'd said. 'Then again, maybe they were one and the same, as far as Nick was concerned.'

Emily's teeth tugged at her lower lip, and her frown was full-blown. 'I didn't know that,' she mumbled, a little disturbed to learn that Nick had been a devoted grandson after all. Somehow it just didn't mesh with the image she had of him.

'Wouldn't it be nice,' Mary asked with sudden brightness, 'if Nick decided to stay on in Random?'

Emily just stared at her, inexplicably terrified by the prospect of such a thing happening. 'He isn't considering that, is he?' she whispered.

Mary shrugged, then her expression softened, and she reached across the table to pat her daughter's hand. This time, Emily knew that the sympathy she saw in those china-doll features was for her, as if she were in some way defective, a poor creature you just had to feel sorry for, because there was some essential part missing.

CHAPTER SIX

NICK was slouched in the front seat of his convertible when Emily opened the shop door the next morning. His head was flung back on the headrest, his eyes were closed, and his jaw was shadowed with the unshaven stubble of his beard. He didn't move at the sound of the door opening, and he didn't move when she clicked it shut behind her.

He's awake, she told herself. He just wants you to think he isn't, so he can pop up and scare you to death.

Lips pursed, she ignored him and started to sweep the pavement, banging the wooden top of the broom more often than necessary on the cement, making as much noise as possible.

Even with the sun barely over the horizon, it was already intolerably hot, and she paused halfway through the chore to wipe her forearm across her brow. Ever so warily, she

108

peered at him from under the cover of her arm, fully expecting to see him upright, one arm flung over the seat back, grinning at her impudently.

He was in precisely the same position, eyes still closed, and the steady rise and fall of his chest marked the unmistakable condition of deep sleep. Random seemed even more quiet than usual; so quiet that she could hear the muted rustle of a single dried leaf skittering across the cement somewhere far up the street.

She jumped at the sharp crack of a door slamming on one of the back streets, shattering the silence, but Nick didn't move.

Emily lowered her arm slowly and looked at him directly, frowning. Her gaze was so intent that she was certain he would somehow sense it and snap upright with a mocking grin—'Caught you, Emily! Caught you looking!'—but after a few seconds of tension it became obvious that that wasn't going to happen, and she relaxed a little, leaning on the broom.

She was going to be nice to Nick today. In spite of everything he'd done to her personally, she was going to make an honest effort to be nice. Ever since her mother had told her how close the two Simon men had been, she'd felt guilty for that awful thing she'd said the first day—the thing about Nick not getting to see his grandfather before he'd died. The words had been cruel enough even without knowing Nick had loved the old man; now the memory of saying them made her cringe. She had to purge the guilt somehow. Maybe she could pretend absolutely nothing had happened between them; that they were meeting for the first time after a ten-year hiatus. She'd ask him how he'd been, what he was doing, where he was living—all the things you were supposed to ask in the polite, controlled conversation of a first meeting.

It would have troubled her greatly to know just how long she stood there looking at him, as motionless as he was, but time seemed to have stopped in the early morning stillness, and she wasn't aware of its passing. Had anyone been around to see it, they might have marvelled at how much Random's Main

Street looked like a still photograph this Saturday, with a single red car at its deserted kerb, the figure of a man slumped inside, the statue of a woman positioned on the pavement close by.

Emily had never dared examine Nick this closely, for fear of being caught at it, and she found the opportunity almost exhilarating — as if she were a smug child performing mischief with absolutely no fear of discovery. The feeling actually made her smile a little, and the smile made her almost beautiful.

He was dressed as casually — as thoughtlessly, really — as he always was, in a plain white T-shirt and faded jeans. His clothes were obviously clean, the T-shirt so white that it was almost blinding, and his hair glittered in the morning sun as if it had just been washed. But his jaw was dark with a day-old beard, and Emily wondered why he would shower and change into fresh clothing, but forget to shave.

Her mouth quirked impatiently to one side. Riddles had always annoyed her. She didn't like unanswered questions, insoluble puzzles. It offended her sense of order.

He stirred slightly in the seat, shifting the position of his pelvis to one side, but even that didn't awaken him. It was strange enough that she'd found him in the car this morning, instead of waiting to pop out at her from some hiding-place, but it was stranger still to find him so deeply asleep. Obviously, he'd had a very hard, very late night.

And then it all came together in her mind, and her face tightened a little. Of course. Just because he loved his grandfather, it didn't automatically make him a saint, any more than becoming a doctor had graced him with dignity. Her eyes narrowed as she focused on the car, coated with dust from one of the dirt roads he'd pretended to avoid so assiduously. He'd probably been out all night, perhaps drinking again as he had that first night; perhaps even looking for 'comfort', as her mother had so naïvely put it, from some other woman. *That* was why he hadn't come back to her apartment again; he'd probably found

more tractable company somewhere else...
like at Crooked Corners over in the next
county, a tavern notorious for loud bands and
willing women and a few upstairs rooms
decent people never talked about.

She scowled at the thought, experiencing
the flash of an unfamiliar feeling she didn't
care to analyse too closely. Quite without intention, she found herself wondering what
kind of woman he'd spent the night with,
what she'd looked like, and then she blew air
sharply out of her nose, disgusted by her own
curiosity.

His head rolled slowly towards her, and he
opened his eyes. They were bloodshot, she
noticed, hoping that he had a brutal hangover.
By now the bruise on his temple had faded to
a sickly greenish-yellow, and she wondered
how he had explained *that* to whomever he
was spending his nights with.

'Well,' he drawled, his mouth curving in a
sleepy smile. 'Can't think of anything I'd
rather see first thing in the morning.'

She banged the head of the broom on the
pavement, raising a cloud of dust. 'It looks

as if you certainly had a good time last night,' she said snidely, turning her head away as if she couldn't bear to look at him.

After a moment he said, 'I see you've decided to exchange silence for sarcasm. It's going to take me a while to decide which is worse.' He chuckled softly when she began to push the broom furiously across a patch of pavement she'd already swept. 'And in answer to your question——'

'I didn't ask a question.'

'And in answer to the question you didn't actually ask, but wanted to...' she could hear the smile in his voice '...I did indeed have a good time last night. One of those rare, rare times that make everything else worth while.'

Her eyes flashed as she banged the broom on the pavement again, then she spun round and stomped into the shop, slamming the door behind her. Whatever he'd done last night was obviously bad enough, without throwing it up in her face, actually *bragging* about it!

Her sandals clattered angrily as she stormed around the counter to fling the broom through the curtained doorway that led to the back room. Lord, her face felt red, and she knew damn well she was ruining everything, letting her outrage show so clearly, but she couldn't seem to control it.

She'd managed to take several deep, calming breaths before Nick got into the shop and over to the counter, but her face was still flushed, and it reddened even further when she saw the amusement in his expression.

'Goodness, Em, you're just as jealous as hell, aren't you?' he grinned, legs spread, thumbs jammed in the front pockets of his jeans.

'In your dreams!' she snapped, glaring at him.

His grin broadened. 'You have every reason to be jealous, of course. I *did* spend last night with a woman—a naked woman...'

Emily blanched, shocked that even he could be so blunt.

'And my one and only regret is that you weren't there with us.'

Her mouth dropped open in disbelief.

'Let me tell you about it, Em——'

'I don't believe it!' she whispered, stunned. 'You're perverted.'

He tried to hold it in, but finally gave up and laughed out loud. 'No, Emily, whatever else you may think I am, I am definitely not a pervert. Even by your rather narrow standards. Let me tell you about last night——'

'No,' she whispered. 'For heaven's sake, no. What kind of a person do you think I am? I don't want to hear this. I *won't* hear this——'

'The naked woman was pregnant,' he inserted quickly.

'What?' Sheer horror was clearly imprinted all over Emily's face, and Nick doubled over the counter, burying his face in his hands, laughing helplessly.

'Emily, Emily,' he gasped. 'She was having a baby. I just happened to be in the right place at the right time, and I helped her deliver it.'

Emily blinked at him, felt her chest jerk in a hitched breath. 'Oh.'

Nick pushed himself up from the counter and dragged his hands over his face, as if he could wipe away the smile that kept cropping up again. 'I was checking out the facilities at Fairfax Hospital when Tommy Hendricks and his wife came in—remember Tommy Hendricks? A tall, skinny guy in our class? Anyway, his wife was in the last stages of labour and the doctor on call hadn't arrived yet, so I lent a hand.'

All she could do was stare at him, even though she knew she must look every bit as foolish as she felt.

'It's what doctors *do*, you know,' he smiled. 'What *I* do.'

Of course she knew that. But she hadn't really pictured it before. Nick Simon, actually practising medicine? Delivering babies? Saving lives?

He sighed distractedly and pushed the fingers of one hand deep into his hair. 'I think you could see birth a million times and still never get over the wonder of it,' he said softly. 'But it's even more incredible when it's someone you know; someone you've known all your life. I never felt that before.'

The wail of the town siren interrupted the first peaceful moment they'd had in days, starting as a low growl, rising steadily in volume and pitch as it climbed to full, ear-splitting power.

Emily's and Nick's heads both jerked simultaneously towards the front window, their faces wiped clean of any expression except worry. Their bodies were similarly tensed, ready. You didn't grow up in the American Midwest without learning early to listen and heed the warning howl of a siren, particularly during the hot, dry months, when its terrifying sound usually meant one of two things, both equally ominous.

Nick was already out of the door, running into the middle of the street, by the time Emily had circumvented the counter. She followed him as fast as she could, her green coat flapping open at her knees. Doors opened up and down the block as other early risers instinctively ran outside to circle the horizon with their eyes.

'Wildfire or tornado?' someone hollered from down the street.

'Don't know yet!' someone else called out an answer.

Even though the street that was deserted just a moment before was gradually filling with people, it was still eerily silent. As if they were mindless robots obeying some universal command from an unseen master, they all turned in slow circles where they stood, shading their eyes with their hands, scanning the sky for either smoke or storm clouds.

'No clouds,' Emily murmured, squinting up at the bleached blue canopy like everyone else. 'It can't be a tornado.'

'No smoke, either,' Nick replied. 'Maybe it's just a small house fire, too far away to see.'

'There!' Herman Belson, owner of the Random Hardware, was twenty yards further down the street, his pudgy finger pointing south between two buildings.

Like a wave rolling on to a beach, the growing crowd surged towards him, all craning their necks to peer at the slice of sky that showed between the buildings. Emily and

Nick were in the centre of the flow, caught in the press of people like the nucleus of a cell. There were at least fifty of them jammed there together, sharing a tiny space on the otherwise empty street, and Emily caught herself marvelling that they had all appeared so quickly from the dark, blank-faced shops and the few second-storey apartments. Somehow she hadn't thought that that many made their homes right on Main Street, just as she did.

'Five miles,' Herman said certainly, staring at the white haze of smoke at the horizon line. 'Mebbe more.'

There was a collective sigh of relief, and Emily could almost feel the subtle relaxation of all the tense bodies around her.

'But it's a big one,' Herman added ominously.

Like a single organism, all heads turned at the sound of the big door on the fire station, one block behind Main Street, rolling up on its massive hinges.

'Looks to be clear over in Fairfax Township,' an elderly male voice came from somewhere behind Emily. 'They must have called our boys for help.'

The undulating wail of the Random Volunteer Fire Department's truck siren pierced the morning air, confirming the statement. A few seconds later the truck's red nose poked around the corner and aimed for the crowd. Like a piece of paper ripped on the dotted line, the crowd parted into two neat halves to give the truck clearance.

'What is it!' Herman called to one of the men standing on the truck's running board, trying to shrug into his gear and hang on at the same time.

'Big swamp fire over by Fairfax!' he called out as they passed. 'Every rig in the county's been called to help! See you all in about two days, if we're lucky!' His voice faded away as the truck picked up speed.

'Another one,' someone muttered, and a grumble rolled through the crowd like the irritated sound of a very large animal.

'Over ten thousand acres gone to fire already,' another voice grumbled. 'Whole damn state's going to burn down if we don't get rain soon.'

A dozen deep-throated assents rumbled through the crowd, and there was something disturbing in the sound. Emily frowned, looking around at the faces she'd known all her life, but had never seen quite this long before. Not that the farmers of Random had never known hard times—the average crop year was never perfect, usually leaning a little to one side of either too wet or too dry—but not since the dust-bowl days of the '30s had the conditions been this extreme, and many of the people here were now facing total devastation. Sometimes that was all it took to wipe out a farm that had been in the same family for generations—one horrendously bad year. It didn't happen often in this part of the country—perhaps once every fifty years—but when it did farming operations tumbled like wobbly dominoes on a board.

'We've gotta have rain!' Wilbur Lindberg shouted, as if there were someone within hearing distance who had rain to give, and was withholding it out of spite. 'I've got three hundred acres of seed blowing away with the topsoil, and my life savings with it!'

Four hundred! Six hundred! Eight hundred! The cries came furiously, as if they were all trying to outdo each other with the size of their potential losses.

Inside, Emily hurt for all of them; all of the people here, and the hundreds of others on farms scattered throughout the county and the state. They were her people, these grim, stalwart farmers whose very lives depended on the fickle whims of the weather; and now their lives were being threatened by circumstances they couldn't control.

In the best of years they still had to battle brush fires, tornadoes, drought, winterkill—and still they persevered. Uneducated, uncultured, unsophisticated, the residents of Random and a thousand Midwestern towns like it were all that—but there was something noble about them, too. Something wonderfully courageous that always made Emily proud to be among their number. But now they were hurting, and there was nothing anybody could do about it.

'I can't remember it ever being this bad,' Nick said into her ear, looking around at the disgruntled faces, catching pieces of a dozen muttered exchanges that were growing louder and louder with the frustration that had been building for months.

'It's never been this bad,' Emily replied dully. 'Not in our lifetime, anyway. A lot of these people are going to lose their farms if we don't get rain soon.' She sighed, as frustrated as everyone else on the street, thinking of her father.

It didn't seem fair that an entire way of life could hinge on something as fickle, something as incidental to the rest of the world as a single rain shower. She wondered how the other segments of the country's population— construction workers, factory workers, doctors, lawyers, teachers—would survive if *their* careers and livelihoods depended on something as unreliable as the weather. They wouldn't, she decided with a grim nod. It took a special kind of courage—or madness—to live with that kind of a shadow over your head.

She felt Nick's warm, dry hand grasp hers at her side, and, perhaps because the despair in the street was almost tangible, the pressure of his fingers was comforting, and she didn't pull away.

'How long since Random's had a rain dance?'

She looked up at him with disbelief. 'You've got to be kidding? I can't even remember the last one. We haven't had a really good crop year here in almost a decade. What's to celebrate?'

His fingers tightened on her hand and he smiled down at her. 'The best parties are never celebrations—ever been to a wake?'

Emily's face hardened and she jerked her hand away. 'You don't party when you're looking disaster right in the eye!' she hissed irritably, looking around quickly to make sure she hadn't been overheard.

'I do.'

'Well you're not one of us!' she said sharply. 'Not any more!'

His head flinched back a little, eyes narrowed as if to ward off a blow. 'A little fun never hurt anyone,' he said carefully, 'and sometimes it even helps; makes waiting out the bad times easier.'

'And sometimes things are so bad that nothing helps,' she said flatly. 'A good time may be a cure-all in the city, but not out here. You've been away too long, Nick.'

After a moment she had to fight the urge to fidget, his gaze made her so uncomfortable.

'I think a good old-fashioned rain dance is just what this town needs, Emily,' he said finally. 'Let's suggest it. You and me. We'll organise it together, get the people——'

Her brows shot up at the idea of being associated with anything so frivolous. 'Don't be ridiculous,' she said, then turned on her heel and started to make her way hurriedly back to her shop.

The crowd had separated into smaller groups, each deeply involved in their own private conversations, each face as dour as the next. Not exactly a gathering primed for dancing in the street, Emily thought with satisfaction. Rain dance, indeed!

She knew the history as well as any farm daughter—the street dance had once been as much a part of Midwestern tradition as silos were a part of the landscape. In Random, back when they had still had them, they had always been called rain dances. As far back as pioneer days settlers had held dances in the street, simply because in those days no town had had a building large enough to host its entire population. Because they were held outside, and therefore limited to the hot, dry summer months when rain was infrequent, the irony of calling them rain dances had apparently appealed to the town's founders, and the label had lasted for generations. But enthusiasm for any celebration had waned with the crop yields during the past decade, and, as far as Emily knew, there hadn't been a street dance in the whole county in years.

And this certainly isn't the summer to resurrect the custom, she thought. Who wanted to dance when crops were dying in the fields and hogs were convulsing in the heat and wildfires were gobbling up huge tracts of the land they lived on?

Sighing, Emily retreated to the workroom at the rear of the store and began the laborious monthly task of scrubbing out the coolers. If there was one saving grace to the morning, it was that Nick hadn't followed her in from the street.

It was almost a full half-hour before the sporadic shouts from outside became loud enough to attract her attention. Curious, she dropped her scrubbing brush in the bucket, wiped her hands on a rag, and passed through the shop to the front door.

The people who had gathered on the street in response to the siren were just now dispersing, *en masse*, oddly enough, instead of in little groups. It looked as if they were all headed for Alfred's Café.

'Guess what, Emily!' Herman Belson called over his shoulder when he caught sight of her. 'We're going to have a rain dance! How about that?'

Emily blinked in disbelief, almost as surprised by the smiles on those previously sullen faces as she was by the preposterous announcement. Finally she lifted her hand in a feeble wave because Herman seemed to expect it, then stared after all of them as they walked away.

She was still standing there, frozen in her doorway, when she heard the sound of a pebble scraping under someone's shoe. Her eyes lifted to the chemist's across the street, seeking motion, seeing none. Finally they focused on Nick, standing directly opposite her, nearly invisible because he was so motionless. He was leaning against a lamppost, hands stuffed in his jeans pockets, his mouth curved in a quiet, mocking smile.

'Got a date for the dance, Emily?' he called out clearly.

CHAPTER SEVEN

THE days grew hotter. Even though it was still May, the lawns in town took on the brown, crisp look of late August, and tree branches drooped towards the ground, as if scanning the dried soil for a drop of moisture. Cattle huddled in barren pastures, tails busily swishing at the early onslaught of summer flies, and Random Creek slowed to a sluggish trickle.

Emily saw all this, and more; but apparently she was the only one. The rest of the town was so caught up in a totally childish frenzy, anticipating that damned street dance, that they barely noticed the earth drying up under their feet. Fools.

She'd stayed in her apartment all day Sunday, sprawled on the floor in front of a fan, trying to concentrate on the shop books. She'd been continually interrupted by phone-calls that excitedly relayed the news of an un-precedented Sunday night town meeting to make plans for the dance. After dark the steady rumble of cars and trucks rolling up to the town hall had filtered in through the open window, and she'd had to turn her television on loud to drown out the noise of mass foolishness.

At least the silly project had distracted Nick enough to give her a little relief from his torment. As a matter of fact, it seemed that he was the only one in town who *hadn't* called her, and Sunday had passed without a sign of him.

But he was waiting outside when she opened the shop on Monday morning, his hair in a boyish tangle, his eyes glinting with mischief. He had sheets of poster-board tucked under one arm, a packet of markers clutched in his hand. 'Signs for the dance,' he explained, his bare arm brushing against her as he pushed his way into the shop. She closed the door and stomped after him, protesting all the way.

'If you think I'm going to make posters for that stupid dance——'

He stopped suddenly and turned, and she brought herself up with a jerk just before she ran right into his chest.

'Of course not. But your shop is the perfect place to do it. God knows the floor is as clean as anyone else's kitchen table, and there's enough room to spread this stuff around. It's what you get for being so compulsively tidy, Emily. When I told them at the meeting I was sure you wouldn't mind——'

'You told them *what*?'

'The town voted unanimously to make your store dance headquarters.' One side of his mouth lifted in a suggestive smirk. 'Of course, we won't be alone much for the next few days, and you'll have to try to keep your hands off me...'

If a customer hadn't chosen precisely that moment to appear, she would have thrown him out on his ear right then, or so she told herself. But that first customer turned into a steady stream of people popping in and out as the day wore on, and it was no longer a question of kicking Nick out of the shop—

she'd have to kick out the whole damn town. At one time or another, almost everyone she knew was sprawled over a piece of posterboard on her green and white floor, diligently lettering under Nick's supervision while she looked on with an owlish glare.

By Tuesday the shop was a shambles, display benches shoved against the wall, poster-board and pens scattered all over the floor, stacks of leaflets teetering in precarious piles on the counter. The bell over the door jingled constantly as people came and went, there was the persistent drone of a dozen conversations going on at once, and order had become chaos. Although Nick was a constant presence, they'd barely exchanged a word. She'd had to satisfy herself with a few well-timed malevolent looks, but he'd only laughed. Emily's composure was as crumpled as the discarded wads of paper cluttering her shop floor.

On Wednesday, she came downstairs a full hour earlier than usual, hoping for a little peace, just a little time to try to straighten the showroom. She looked around at the mess and sighed helplessly, not knowing where to start. For two days now she hadn't been able to perform the morning cleaning ritual, the place was so cluttered, and today, apparently, would be no exception.

'Damn you anyway, Nick Simon,' she muttered, but there was no real feeling in her tone. He'd robbed her of her reputation, her privacy, and now even her shop; and anger seemed so feeble against such a list of transgressions that it was suddenly pointless. To hell with it. To hell with *him*. All this would be over soon enough; today, in fact.

She jumped at the sound of tapping on the door window, then sighed in resignation. If she didn't let him in, he'd probably just jump through the plate-glass window.

'You're down early,' he grinned as he brushed by her on the way inside. He was wearing snug jeans and a white dress-shirt that clearly belonged under an expensive suit jacket. The sleeves were rolled halfway up his browned forearms, and for some reason Emily found that more disquieting than the revealing T-shirts and tank-tops he favoured in the heat.

She covered her uneasiness by sniping at him. 'If I come down any later than this, I have to stand in line to get into my own shop.'

He stopped halfway towards the counter and frowned at her over his shoulder. 'The past two days have really been tough on you, haven't they, Emily?' he asked quietly. For once, there was no mockery in his voice. 'I guess I never thought about it before, but all this activity must be a nightmare for someone who loves order as much as you do. I don't suppose it's doing much for your business, either.'

Emily was about to accept the commiseration as her due when she frowned suddenly, remembering the receipts from the last two days. Her sanity might be at risk, but sales had sky-rocketed with all the extra traffic. She looked down and brushed prissily at the front of her green coat. 'Well,' she admitted grudgingly, 'business hasn't really been *that* bad...'

His face broke into an immediate smile. 'Great. Glad to hear it, because you'll probably be getting a lot more traffic through here between now and the dance.'

Her eyes jerked up sharply. 'You said today was the last day you'd be working in here. You *promised*.'

'And I keep my promises,' he was quick to say. 'But . . .' he left the sentence unfinished, and turned to walk rapidly to the counter.

'But *what*?' she demanded, hurrying after him.

His forearms were braced on the formica as he stared at the back wall.

'Ni-ick . . .' she drew his name out into a two-syllable warning, and he handed her a sheet of paper without looking at her.

'What's this?' she mumbled suspiciously, frowning down at it.

'Just the leaflet advertising the dance,' he said innocently, but he still wouldn't look at her. 'It's going all over the county this afternoon.'

She sighed impatiently and scanned the sheet, then flapped it at him. 'So? What's this got to do with me?'

'Read the bottom line.'

She grimaced and found the large print at the bottom, then began to read aloud. ' "All proceeds to benefit the Random Fire Department. Tickets can be purchased at" . . . *what*? "Tickets can be purchased at the" . . . "the Random Flower Shop?" What *is* this?'

Finally he looked at her. Sheepishly. And then he shrugged. 'You had the ideal location. You're right in the middle of the block.'

'Dammit, Nick, you can't do this! I'm running a business here, not a ticket booth for your stupid dance! You erase that right now!'

'Can't.'

'What do you mean, you can't? You *can*, and you'd *better*.'

'Wouldn't make any difference if I did. We've already got a hundred posters out that say the same thing.' He moved quickly to grab the leaflet from her hands, sensing that she was about to rip it down the middle.

Her hands snatched at empty air, then fell to her sides and clenched into fists. She felt her face reddening, her whole body starting to tremble. A hundred posters...

'I won't do it,' she whispered, trying so hard to keep from screaming that she over-compensated. Her voice was barely audible. 'First you donate my shop—*my* shop—for this...this...art project, and now you've got me selling tickets! What's next? Am I singing with the band, too?'

He smiled with delighted surprise. 'To tell you the truth, I never thought of that. Can you sing, Emily?'

She blew a frustrated blast of air out of her cheeks and clenched her fists even tighter to keep from punching him on the nose.

'Oh, come on, Em.' He reached out to touch her face and she jerked her head to the side. 'A little community involvement will do you good. It's probably just what you need to bring you out of your shell——'

'I'm not in a shell! And I don't need you to tell me what I need!'

'Of course you do,' he replied, completely unruffled. 'You need me for that, and a whole lot more.'

She just stared at him, her mouth open, her eyes wide. It just didn't seem possible that any one man was capable of that much conceit. She hitched in a furious breath, and forced herself to speak in a steady, controlled monotone. 'What I need is for you to go back where you came from,' she said quietly. 'To leave me and my business and my town alone. The happiest day of my life will be the day I see the last of you.'

He looked at her for a moment, and, although for days she'd wanted nothing more than to wipe that cocky smile off his face, now that she'd finally managed to do it she wasn't quite as satisfied as she'd thought she would be.

He stared straight at her for the longest time, then he cocked his head, apparently searching for something in her face. She kept her eyes focused and narrow, her mouth in a rigid line, but he must have imagined he saw something other than the chill she was trying so hard to project, because his cheeks suddenly dimpled in a knowing smile.

'You're going to miss me when I go, Emily.' He said it like a prophecy. 'You're going to lie up there on your back in your little old-maid bed, and you're going to wish I were there, with my hands all over you.'

Emily gasped audibly, the size of the breath caught in her throat threatening to choke her.

Nick's smile just broadened, then he rolled the leaflet into a tube and walked towards the door.

She closed her eyes and breathed deeply after the door closed behind him. She had to stop letting him see how much he disturbed her. That was the obvious reason for his behaviour, of course. He was like a little boy, taking perverted pleasure from saying things just for their shock value. The trick was to ignore him, like any other pest, then maybe he'd leave her alone.

She was still breathing hard. Suddenly she became conscious of her breasts pushing up the light green fabric as they rose and fell, and she frowned hard and willed them to stop. 'You're going to wish I were there, with my hands all over you...'

Her eyes fell closed in a motion that was more despair than outrage, and she tried to concentrate on the blessed silence of her little shop while she still had it. Lord, she mused, it's so peaceful when he's not around. So restful. That's all I want. Just a little peace.

She sagged against the counter, her lips trying for a smile, but after a few seconds the smile faltered a little as the first silence she'd experienced in days began to irritate her. A few seconds more, and she began to frown, then drum her fingers on the counter-top.

Had the shop ever been this quiet?

She jerked her head around at the jangle of the little bell over the door, then felt something very close to relief when a knot of chattering people came in. Without realising it, she smiled.

By ten o'clock the shop was crowded with a dozen people hunched over the counter, crouched on the floor, all labouring over the last of the posters. There was an undercurrent of chatter, frequent giggles, and, occasionally, uproarious laughter as some preposterous comment made the rounds.

After that first impulsive smile of greeting, Emily remembered to frown disapprovingly at the nonsense going on around her. Almost everyone here certainly had something better to do—something more productive than huddling over a poster like a child with a new box of crayons. What was Mr Tollefson doing off the farm, his gnarled old hand clutching a marker instead of the gear lever on a tractor? And wasn't this the day Mrs Hoeffer's bridge group met for needlework? And yet here they were, a collection of fussy old ladies apparently having the time of their lives, if their giggling was any measure. Even young John Clauson and his wife had stolen a few hours from their dairy farm to come in, and they were as hard-working and reclusive a pair as lived in the township.

As the morning wore on, her disapproval gave way to resigned tolerance. Let them fritter away their valuable time on such frivolous pursuits. It wasn't her concern. She, at least, was bent earnestly over the shop books; she, at least, was accomplishing something worthwhile. 'The only sane person left in the whole town,' she muttered down at her ledger.

'What did you say, Emily?' Mrs Hoeffer piped up.

Emily's head jerked up and she forced a businesslike smile. 'Oh, nothing. Just talking to myself.'

'Well, come on, dear. Try your hand at this.'

Emily's smile weakened when she saw the piece of blank poster-board Mrs Hoeffer was holding towards her. She stared at it as if it were a poisonous snake, ready to strike. ''Uh . . . no . . . I don't think so . . .'

'Oh, come on. It's *fun*.'

Her smile twitched nervously, and she felt an odd fluttering in her stomach. Suddenly someone shoved a blue marker into her hand,

and every muscle in her body tensed. Permitting this craziness in her shop was one thing; participating in it was something else altogether—something no one would have expected of her a few days ago.

'Here you go, Emily.' John Clauson and his wife were pushing their materials to one side, making an empty space between them on the floor. They both looked up at her with expectant smiles. Did they actually think she was going to get down there and colour and giggle with the rest of them? What was wrong with these people? Didn't they remember who she was?

At noon, a large shadow blocked the light from the door and everyone looked up from their work. The silhouette of Nick's form looked massive, wrenchingly masculine, standing there with his legs spread and arm muscles bulging under the weight of the crate he carried. 'I've got two dozen hamburgers, a mess of fries, and a case of pop in here, if anyone's interested,' he said, and there was a chorus of hungry voices. 'Where's Emily?'

His glance scanned the shop, passing right over her.

'Here.' Her hand shot up automatically, then froze in mid-air when she realised what she must look like. The rising temperature had made her discard the green overall over an hour ago, and now she sat cross-legged on the floor in only shorts and a sleeveless blouse, a half-finished poster propped on her lap.

Nick's blue eyes found her voice, passed on without a pause, then snapped back in a double take. She looked away quickly, smoothing the short blonde hair behind her ears as if that would somehow make her appearance more dignified.

'Emily?' His voice pulled at her eyes. The colour deepened in her already flushed cheeks as his eyes wandered down her bare arms to her legs, then lifted slowly to her face again.

A smudge of dirt made an angle of his cheekbone, strands of his own blond hair clung damply to his brow, and his white shirt hung open, revealing an avenue of tanned chest and stomach that made Emily's hand whiten around the marker it held.

He pulled his eyes away reluctantly, passed out food and drink to everyone else first, then hunkered down next to her and pushed the box of food between them. His smile was mischievous, but his eyes were strangely intense when they locked on to hers.

'Who the hell are you?' his voice rumbled in a tease too low to be overheard by the others.

She frowned and grabbed a can of pop from the box. Ignore him, she reminded herself. Just pretend he doesn't exist.

'Certainly not Earnest Emily,' he goaded her. 'That woman would never crawl around on a dirty floor and show *that* much leg, let alone help make posters for a stupid town dance.'

She tried not to blush at the reference to her legs; tried even harder not to bristle at the sarcasm in his tone. 'The sooner the posters get finished, the sooner I'll have my shop back,' she said in defence of her behaviour.

He grinned, somehow making fun of her explanation without saying a word. She sniffed and looked away, and the next thing she knew he'd dropped from his crouch to sit cross-legged right next to her, his jeans-clad knee pressed against her bare one. She sidled a little to the left, and he followed.

'Stop that!' she hissed out of the side of her mouth.

His knee pushed more insistently against hers, and now she felt the tickling brush of his shirt-sleeve against her arm as he leaned towards her.

Ignore him, ignore him, she reminded herself firmly, so intent on her concentration that she missed his head bending towards her ear. His breath fluttered like the wings of a moth against the sensitive skin of her neck, raising goose-bumps. 'You have beautiful legs,' he whispered. 'I'd like to kiss them.'

Emily twisted her head away, blushing so hard that her eyes almost started to water.

'You keep leaning towards John like that, and he's going to think you're coming on to him.'

She jerked her eyes to the left, saw John Clauson's arm a fraction of an inch from her shoulder, and jerked herself straight, bumping Nick in the process.

'Not so rough, Em!' he said loudly, and someone behind her tittered.

She glared straight ahead at nothing, gritting her teeth so tightly together that her jaw ached. I'll kill him, she thought calmly. I'll just have to kill him. That's all there is to it.

Somehow she found the presence of mind to reach for a hamburger, unwrap it, and take a bite that tasted like sawdust. She could feel him watching her from the side, but steadfastly refused to look at him, pretending great interest in the tasteless food she was trying to force down.

Finally, out of the corner of her eye, she saw his legs unfold and tuck beneath him as he rose. At the last minute, he bent to whisper, 'Be careful, Emily. It's starting to look suspiciously as if you're having a good time. A thing like that could destroy your image.'

Before her lips could form the first word of a retort she hadn't even composed yet, he was clapping his hands for attention. 'OK, people. You've got two more hours before school lets out, then we'll have a gang of kids to distribute all this artwork. Finish as many as you can.'

She cringed visibly when his hand ruffled the short hair on the top of her head with a casualness that implied he did it often.

'I'll see *you* later,' he added, just before walking away.

There wasn't a person in the shop who didn't draw the obvious conclusion from that remark, and as Emily saw all the conspiratorial grins on all those faces she wondered if it were actually possible for someone to die of embarrassment.

'You two are so cute,' Kathy Clauson chuckled, stabbing a French fry into her mouth.

Emily looked over at her, dumbfounded. How could these people be so blind? Couldn't they see what was really going on here?

It was the first time she really understood how much her image had changed since

Nick's arrival. As far as these people were concerned, she was no longer the earnest, solitary, rather uninteresting town florist. In their imaginations, at least, she was now a fascinating half of a wildly romantic twosome, an object of curiosity and gossip and wistful speculation. *That* was why they'd been so certain she would join in the silly poster brigade. They didn't think of her as Earnest Emily any more. They thought she was the woman whom Nick Simon had made up.

She looked around at all the friendly faces smiling at her, and realised that this, at last, was her chance to set the record straight. She could tell them the truth right now: that the only night Nick had spent in her apartment, he'd spent passed out on the couch; that there wasn't a shred of truth to the fantasy relationship he'd let the whole town believe they were having; that she was not having some stormy affair; that, in fact, she was the same old steady, quiet, slightly prudish Emily Swenson she'd always been...

She looked down briefly, sighed with determination, then stood up and faced her audience. Tell them, she told herself. Tell them right now.

'Well,' she said after a moment of stomach-rolling anticipation, and then for some reason her mouth refused to form the words her brain was dictating. She just stood there with everyone staring at her, paragraphs forming in her mind while her lips remained mute. *Tell them!* her thoughts shrieked inside her head. Or for the rest of your life they're going to think you're someone you're not, someone you've never been, and could never hope to be. You don't want *that* to happen, do you?

The words popped out like a cork under pressure. 'If two hours are all we've got,' she said, 'we'd better get back to work.'

CHAPTER EIGHT

NICK came back to the shop in the late afternoon, followed by a caravan of wildly diverse vehicles—old, unpainted pick-up trucks, flashy hot rods, and even a few classic convertibles, every bit as flamboyant as his own. Each vehicle was crammed with exuberant high-school students who spilled out on to the pavement and then into the flower shop, and the noise level swelled with their animated chatter.

Emily was behind the counter when they came in, helping Mr Tollefson stack the completed posters. She looked up and frowned at the sudden, alien infusion of youthful energy into her normally staid environment.

'All right, kids!' Nick called out over the noise, and if it hadn't been for his physical maturity he would have been indistinguishable from the students. The way he

moved, the enthusiasm in his voice, everything about him seemed terribly young at that
moment, and the students seemed to sense
that. They gathered around him like groupies.
'You've all got your assignments! Grab your
posters and leaflets and start your routes. Remember, the more people we pull from other
townships, the more money for Random's
Fire Department!'

Emily's shoulders lifted in a heavy sigh as
she watched the kids bustle around like
revving engines, excess energy and high spirits
exaggerating every move, and suddenly she
felt older than she had in a long time. The
old line about never being that young, even
when she was that young, kept running
through her mind, and soon she found herself
resenting the students, and resenting Nick,
too, because he seemed every bit as young as
they did.

Her mouth tightened as she watched the
girls cluster around him, more than one
pausing to touch his arm, to ask a wide-eyed
question, to bat a long-lashed eye. A partic-

ularly winsome brunette tossed her long hair so that it brushed Nick's shoulder, and Emily absently reached up to touch her own closely cropped blonde hair, frowning.

He just loves this, she thought, her features hardening as she watched him respond to the girls. When one of them grabbed his hands and babbled something in excitement, he actually gave her a quick hug, laughing at whatever she'd said.

Everyone was too busy to notice Emily standing there quietly, her expression flattening, her posture growing more rigid and aloof by the minute.

Gradually the shop began to clear as students filtered out to begin their delivery routes, and poster-makers were finally free to go home and attend to other chores. Eventually Emily and Nick were the only ones left: she still behind the counter, he standing in the middle of the shop, watching her. She glanced at him briefly, saw that his open shirt clung damply to his body in the heat, that the gold of his hair had been dulled by blowing dust.

'I'm proud of you, Emily. You actually loosened up a little today. Got down there on the floor with the natives and did something absolutely useless, just because it felt good.'

She made a face, then dropped her eyes and pretended to study an old cash-register receipt someone had left on the counter.

'Alone at last,' he said quietly.

Emily pursed her lips without looking up.

'There's no reason for you to be jealous of a bunch of high-school girls, you know.'

Her head jerked up and her face flooded with colour. 'Don't flatter yourself.'

'I'm not. You are.'

She made a disgusted face and started clearing the day's debris off the counter.

'Not that I'm objecting, mind you,' he said with a chuckle, approaching the counter and resting his arms on it. She didn't have to look at him to know he was smiling. She could hear it in his voice. 'I like it when you're jealous. You can shoot daggers all the way across a room with those green eyes of yours.'

Emily grabbed a rag and started polishing furious circles on the formica. 'You've got an imagination to match your ego,' she said icily. 'I couldn't care less what you do, or with whom.'

His hand shot down to cover hers, and she froze, the rag still clutched in her hand, her hand clutched in his. 'Oh, you care all right,' he said quietly. 'You're just not ready to admit it yet. Maybe not even to yourself.'

Emily frowned down at her hand, wondering why it hadn't jerked away as she'd told it to. It looked small and pale and helpless, trapped beneath the broad, darker span of his. For a moment she forgot herself, and was mesmerised by the sharply defined lines of his tendons, tracking from wrist to knuckles.

'You know,' he murmured, 'your mouth drives me crazy.'

Shocked by the intimate quality of his voice, her eyes snapped up and collided with his. Almost instinctively, she sucked her lips inwards.

'Oh, Em...' he chuckled deep in his throat '...when you finally let go, it's going to blow me away.'

She took a shallow, shaky breath, then remembered to pull her hand from beneath his and look away. Not the least bit discouraged, he hopped sideways on to the counter and smiled down at her over his right shoulder. 'It was your mouth that got to me in the first place, you know, all the way back in high school.'

Emily started polishing circles again, her eyes riveted to her rag.

'You were always so damn prim and proper, collars buttoned up to your chin, face pursed up like a prune, as defensive as hell—that keep-away look you wore all the time was like a blast of cold air from a freezer...' He paused and sighed. 'But sometimes—not often, but sometimes—the look slipped. Like in Mr Barker's history class. You just loved that class, didn't you?'

She glanced up suspiciously, wondering how he knew that—it was the second time he'd surprised her by knowing things she hadn't thought anyone knew. She realised too late that she shouldn't have looked up at all.

Once her eyes met his, she couldn't seem to pull them away...

'And whenever you got really involved in what old Barker was saying...well, your eyes would go soft and that mouth...' he took a quick breath '...that mouth of yours would just...unfold. Like a flower.' His gaze shifted downwards to her lips, the blue of his eyes seemed to grow darker, and his voice became husky. 'Just like now.'

She was staring at him, her lips unconsciously parted, her eyes growing wider by the second. She couldn't remember when she'd breathed last. As she watched, his nostrils flared slightly, and his tongue passed over his lower lip.

'There's a softness in you, Emily. There always has been. You just knock yourself out trying to hide it, but little hints of it keep rising to the surface—like when you stopped to smell the black-eyed Susans every day— and when I kissed you for the very first time.' His eyes fell closed at the memory, and his head tipped slightly to one side, as if the memory itself were still just a little beyond belief. His voice dropped even lower. 'It was like . . . being burned.' He opened his eyes and looked deeply into hers. 'I've kissed a lot of women since then, Em, but it never felt the same. I didn't think it ever would again—I thought it was just one of those moments in your past that your memory distorts all out of proportion. Then I saw you again that first day I was in town, and I had to find out; I had to find out for sure. And that night in your apartment . . . I did.'

Emily was sure that if she stood there for one second longer, trapped by the blue fire in his eyes and hypnotised by his voice, she would simply burst into flame. She blinked, snapped her mouth closed, then dropped quickly to her knees behind the counter and pretended to start straightening the shelves.

Almost before she could register the motion, he'd swung his legs over and was standing with his legs spread next to where she knelt. Instantly she was at a disadvantage, on her knees before him like a supplicant; but at the very moment when the muscles in her legs tightened to rise he said clearly from above her, 'Get up, Emily,' and that made rising just an obedient response to his command. No way was she going to do that.

'Maybe you're right.' He dropped to his knees suddenly, facing her. 'This is better. No one passing by can see us if we're down here.'

Now she could get up. But just as she reached for the top of the counter, he grabbed her wrists and turned her on her knees, then pulled her so sharply against him that her teeth clicked together.

With as much disdain as her position would allow, she raised her eyes slowly and said, 'Are you going to try the forceful man bit *again*?'

Amazingly, he just laughed, pulling at her wrists until her fingers were forced open to splay across his chest. 'If you like,' he smiled, flattening his hands over hers. 'Feel that, Emily?'

Her eyes flashed, but of course she did. The hard, steady beat of his heart pumped against her palms. 'Feel what?' She arched one brow, but the effect was lost when her voice cracked.

'My heart,' he whispered, 'beating as fast as yours.'

His eyes dropped immediately to her throat, and she realised with something like horror that he was staring at the pulse-point there; that no matter how chilling her tone, how contemptuous her expression, that pulse in the hollow of her throat was going to give her away if she couldn't manage to control it.

He leaned into her slightly, until they were pressed tightly together from knee to shoulder, with only the fold of her arms between them. She felt the hard ridge of his thighs against hers, watched his brows twitch and his eyes flicker, and then saw the delicate flare of his nostrils and the slight tightening of the skin beneath his eyes.

Oh, please don't let that be happening to my face, she thought frantically. Please don't let it be that obvious.

'Feel it,' he commanded hoarsely, his voice deadly serious now. His head rolled back slightly; his eyes impaled hers through narrowed lids.

Her pulse leaped, forcing her green eyes wide, and her breath caught silently in her throat. Sit down, she told her body. Sit back on your heels, away from him; but the moment she tried, his hands released her wrists and clutched at her lower back, pulling her into him. Fingers kneaded at either side of her spine, making it arch, then crawled upwards, sealing her torso to his, inch by inch.

When his fingers threaded through her short hair and his palms covered her ears, she heard the waves of an ocean she had never seen pounding on a distant shore. When his thumbs prodded her chin upwards, she felt the pulse of his breath like a hot tropical breeze.

'Don't,' she breathed, but his mouth came down firmly on her parted lips, absorbing the word and the protest right out of existence.

There were too many sensations, racing from millions of nerve-endings across a baffling, complex circuitry that went absolutely haywire in her brain. For separate flashes of time, certain signals stood out from the rest, so intensely clear that they demanded total attention—like right *now*—the sound of his breath breaking against her cheek; and, in the next instant, the slick warmth of his tongue searching for hers; and in the next the unmistakable hardness grinding into her hips, making her breath catch and her head feel incredibly heavy.

Without any warning at all, his hands dropped to grip her upper arms, and his face buried itself beneath her chin, tongue working at the hollow of her throat, then trailing downwards into the opening of her blouse. She felt his teeth graze her skin as he bit down on one side of her blouse and jerked his head to the side. She barely heard the tiny clatter of buttons skittering across the floor over the harsh sound of his breathing, and even if the thought that he had ruined yet another blouse had registered, it wouldn't have made any difference, because now he was kissing the swollen rise of her breast, and now his tongue was whisking beneath the lace top of her bra, and now he was tugging urgently at the strap...and then his mouth closed over the tip of her bared breast and she fell into him helplessly, feeling the tug of his lips pull something hot and seething all the way up from her stomach.

He groaned once against her flesh, then raised his head and looked right into her eyes. His mouth was open, his lips wet, and he pulled in air with a rasping sound. His eyes looked black. He filled his hand with her breast, and when he pressed against it lightly her eyes slammed shut and a tiny sound crawled up from her throat.

'Come on, Em. We're going upstairs,' he growled. 'Right now.'

And there it was again. The masculine command, demanding feminine obedience; the most loathsome thing imaginable, to become subservient to another, to let the desires of the body rule the logic of the mind; but oh, she wanted to go.

Nick reached up and ran his finger over her lips until they parted helplessly. '*Now*, Emily,' he said in a stranger's voice, and a shudder passed through her body, evidence of her last futile struggle in a war she knew she had lost.

'Hey, Nick!' The shout and the bell over the door shattered the silence simultaneously, and they both froze behind the counter, staring at each other with wide-flown eyes. 'Hey Nick! You in here?'

Emily slammed her hand over her mouth so she wouldn't cry out. It felt like the bottom of her stomach had fallen to the floor.

It was Herman from the hardware store next door, and any second now he was going to stomp across the floor and peer over the counter and see her cringing here half-naked...

The vision was so horrifying she couldn't imagine its ending; the fear of discovery was so great that she didn't dare move, even to cover herself. For one miserable moment, she thought she was going to lose control entirely and just burst into tears.

Nick frowned hard at her, then suddenly called out, 'I'm here!' and popped upright from behind the counter. One of his hands pressed down firmly on top of her head, and his right foot nudged her hip, forcing her into the cubby-hole right beneath the cash register.

Even in her quiet panic, she had enough presence of mind to be surprised by his actions. After all his efforts to convince the town that she was having a scandalous affair with him, now that it was close to being the truth he was actually trying to spare her the embarrassment. Something about that just didn't make sense, but she was too distraught to dwell on it.

'Herman!' she heard him say from above her, and it seemed impossible that Herman wouldn't notice the thick breathiness of his voice and know precisely what had been going on. 'I'm just putting some of this stuff away for Emily. What's up?'

He was stacking something on the counter, making enough noise to cover her movements. She pressed even deeper into her hiding-place, tugging her bra up and her blouse closed.

'Nothing, really,' Herman replied. 'Where is Emily?'

'Oh, she went upstairs a little while ago...' his voice became lighter, conveying a message only she would understand '...to change her blouse, I think.'

She rolled her eyes and reached out to pinch his leg, then jerked her hand back, aghast at what she'd been about to do. It was such a...*playful* gesture, so incredibly out of character that Nick would probably have fainted dead away from shock, then Herman would have had to rush behind the counter to pick him up, then he'd have seen staid old Emily folded into a ball with her blouse hanging open, and then *he* would have fainted dead away...

She squeezed her eyes shut and suppressed an insane giggle. A moment ago she'd been ready to burst into tears of humiliation. Now, with the danger of imminent discovery over, the whole situation seemed suddenly hilarious. Here she was, stuffy old Emily Swenson—*half-naked*, stuffy old Emily

Swenson, she amended—jammed into a cramped hiding-place like a high-school girl trying not to get caught in the boys' locker-room. She didn't know which was worse: that she'd got herself into such a situation in the first place, or that she was actually beginning to enjoy it.

She clamped a hand over her mouth, feeling devilish and young and terribly adven-turous—and then, suddenly, a little sad, be-cause she was twenty-seven years old and she'd never felt those things before.

'Well, I really stopped by to catch you before you left town, Nick,' Herman said. 'Just wanted to say goodbye.'

Slowly, ever so slowly, the words pene-trated Emily's brain, and the whole world seemed to grind to a halt. Her hand fell away from her mouth, and her smile faded.

'Oh.' Nick's voice sounded lame. 'You didn't have to do that, Herman. Nice of you, though.'

'Well, wish you didn't have to go. Lord knows you'll be missed. Any idea when you'll be coming back?'

Emily held her breath while Nick cleared his throat. 'Not really, Herman. Nothing definite.'

For a moment, the floor seemed to shift slightly under her, and she felt dizzy. He's leaving. He's leaving Random, and his last act was going to be the promised seduction of the town spinster. He was going to take me up-stairs and ... and all the time he was planning that, he knew that he was leaving. Her lower lip almost disappeared and she had to remind herself to blink.

Of course he's leaving, some rational part of her mind muttered. What did you think? That he'd pop back into town after a ten-year absence and put down roots? That this va-cation would simply go on forever? He had to go back to his real life eventually. You knew that. You just ... forgot.

A long splinter was pulling away from the wood divider, right at Emily's eye-level. She focused on it, reached for it absently, and started to work it away from the wood. Herman and Nick were exchanging small talk above her, but their voices receded to a distant drone. A cramp was threatening to seize her right calf, but the sensation was recorded in such a remote corner of her brain that she hardly noticed it. She was too intent on the splinter. Nothing else in the world existed, except that single fragment of wood; and nothing seemed quite as important as removing it.

'Emily?'

She snapped to awareness and bumped her head on the shelf above her. Nick's crouching form was a peripheral shadow on her left, and she turned her head slowly to look at it. He was smiling. Dammit, he was smiling.

'You can come out now. He's gone.'

She looked down at the tangle of her legs with a glazed, stupid expression, as if she couldn't imagine how they'd got there; then absently forced her numbed muscles to unfold. She emerged from the cubby-hole on hands and knees, and that seemed horribly appropriate.

'Here. Let me help you up.'

She ignored his hand and pulled herself up by the counter-top, then remained standing there, facing the front of the store. She stared at the door as if she could already see him walking through it, and spoke without looking at him. 'You're leaving,' she said dully.

'Not for an hour,' he leaned to whisper playfully in her ear. She was too numb to pull away. 'We've got an hour.'

The sheer callousness of his response left her stunned. Her head turned slowly until their eyes met. His were intensely blue, sparkling with anticipation; hers were a chilling, flat green.

She kept trying to tell herself how lucky she was. She'd been totally out of control, her body responding without the direction of her mind, and Herman's interruption was all that had saved her from becoming exactly what her mother was—what she had sworn she would never be—a woman commanded by a man, ruled by a man, controlled by a man.

The realisation of how close she had come made her shudder. How horrible it was to learn after all these years that strength of will was just an illusion; that locked somewhere within her body was an automatic weakness, just waiting to betray her the moment a man pushed the right buttons. She hadn't lost control—she'd almost *given* it away, to a man who would have been watching the clock, no less, counting off the minutes of a single hour.

'Emily?' He was looking at her strangely, trying to read the expressionless mask she wore.

'You're very good, Nick,' she said calmly, looking up at him. 'I underestimated you.'

He went perfectly still, his eyes riveted on her face.

'I was actually going to go to bed with you,' she continued, her voice so devoid of emotion that it sounded mechanised.

Nick watched her carefully for a moment, his eyes suddenly wary. 'There's nothing wrong with that, Emily,' he finally said, very softly. 'When two people——'

'Everything's wrong with that, Nick, because the reasons were all wrong. I didn't plan it, I didn't think about it, I just...' she could barely force out the words '...lost control.' When she raised her eyes, she looked beaten, defeated. 'I didn't even know that could happen to women,' she added in the pathetic voice of a bewildered child.

Slowly, as if he were afraid she would bolt at the slightest movement, he reached up and took her shoulders in his hands. 'But, Emily, that's the best part——'

'No!' she whispered, her eyes a little wild.

His fingers tightened on her shoulders, but only slightly. 'It's part of giving, Emily.' He bent at the knees to peer directly into her eyes. 'Part of relating. You lose a little control when someone gets close, but it's worth it.'

'No,' she whispered, shaking her head slowly. 'I don't want that. Ever.'

'Em...' he frowned so hard that the line over his nose looked etched there '...you've been in control all your life. It's all you've ever had. Let it go. You're running out of time.'

In the space of a single blink, her eyes hardened. 'Am I, Nick? Is my hour almost up?'

His lips tightened in exasperation. 'That's not what I meant, and you know it,' he said, a little more sharply than he had intended. 'Dammit, Emily!' He dropped his hands from her shoulders and looked down at them, frustrated. 'Ask me to stay,' he said quietly, still looking down. 'That's all you have to do. Just ask me to stay.'

Her brow twitched a little. It sounded like such a simple, harmless thing, just asking him to stay... but it wasn't simple, and it wasn't harmless. As long as he was around, she was at constant risk. All he had to do was touch her, look at her, and she'd be back behind the counter again, ready to subjugate her will to his, ready to move when he called and follow where he led, because he had that power over her, that power she didn't understand and couldn't fight, and she would only be safe if he just left.

'I don't want you to stay,' she said firmly, her voice suddenly back at full strength.

Every nuance of expression bled from his face as he stared at her, and in the sudden silence the echo of her words hung in the air like a death knell.

He stared at her for a very long time, and as she watched his eyes seemed to empty of colour until they were a pale, glassy, doll-like blue. Finally he sighed and ran one hand back through his hair, leaving darker tracks in the sun-bleached blond.

She couldn't really remember his turning away, stepping through the clutter of discarded posters and papers on his way to the door. One minute he was standing in front of her, and the next, it seemed, he was all the way across the room with his hand on the knob, half turned to look back at her.

His right arm was knotted with the force of his grip, and a dark slice of chest and stomach showed between the parted halves of his shirt. His face was in shadow, but his hair caught all the light coming in through the door, and it looked like a crown of white fire. Oddly enough, Emily knew even then that this was the way she would remember him—not laughing, teasing, blue eyes alight with mockery and mischief, but like this: half in shadow, blond hair flaming with an unearthly light, and silent.

'You're going to miss me, Em,' he said quietly.

She felt her lips tighten convulsively as the door closed behind him. The latch fell into its notch with a faint click, but the sound reverberated in her mind like the slamming of a prison-cell door.

CHAPTER NINE

HE'S gone.

It was the very first thought in Emily's mind when she woke the morning after Nick left town, and for a moment it paralysed her. As long as she was trapped in that netherworld between sleep and full wakefulness, that place where feelings ruled before the mind kicked into gear, she felt the full, brutal weight of desolation bearing down. Thankfully, the moment passed quickly, and her orderly mind pushed ridiculous notions like actually missing Nick Simon back into the shadows where they belonged. Why should she miss him, after all? Did you miss a toothache? An itchy cast on a broken arm? And that was all he was, really, just one of those constant, inescapable irritations in life that left a strange emptiness when you were finally free of them.

She made her bed, started the coffee, showered and started to dress, grumbling automatically as she tugged on the straps of the confining bra. The second strap was halfway up her arm when her hand jerked to a stop, and she remembered that she wouldn't have to wear the hated thing any more. There wouldn't be anyone to notice.

She tried to smile as she shoved it back into the drawer, then saw in the mirror that the smile looked fake. Irritated by her own reaction, she snatched a lipstick and started to put it on. She'd dragged the coral gloss halfway across her lower lip when she remembered what Nick had said about her mouth, and her lip trembled. Furious, she flung the tube down without finishing and grabbed her hairbrush to slick her short blonde strands in place with vicious, impatient strokes. 'I like your hair like that,' his voice rumbled from the back of her mind, and the brush clattered to the floor as she stood rigidly in front of the mirror, her eyes slammed shut—eyes he thought looked like spring, she remembered involuntarily. Dammit! Wasn't there *any-thing* in her life that wouldn't remind her of him?

She poured coffee—just as she'd poured coffee for him that night he'd shown up drunk; she fluffed the cushions on the couch—the couch where she had first felt his mouth on hers; and finally, desperate to escape, she literally ran down the narrow steps to the workroom, through the door to the shop proper, and came face to face with a flood of memories—so many memories, from such a short span of time.

She walked the length of the counter as if in a trance, trailing her fingers on the cool formica, remembering the times he had hopped up to sit there, the way his forearms had looked braced on its edge, the un-speakable things she had felt crouched behind it before Herman had come in . . .

Her eyes lifted slowly to the door, and she imagined she could see him there still, standing with his hand on the knob, his shadowed gaze touching her all the way across the room . . .

Her eyes fell closed briefly, then opened again to focus on that place outside where the flashy red convertible had become a fixture, as much a part of Main Street as Nick Simon had become a part of her life. As she stared at the empty space, she felt a sharp, almost physical pain in her chest.

'You'll miss me, Em,' he'd warned her, and oh, it wasn't fair that she did. She hadn't even *liked* him, really. He was too flip, too sure of himself, and, above all, too…controlling. Good heavens. He'd only been in town a couple of weeks, and in that time he'd managed to turn the whole place upside-down, and her along with it. How could you possibly like a man like that? And—an even more frightening question—how could she have felt the things she had for such a man? They had names for women like that, didn't they?

A shudder passed through her as her body remembered the things her mind was trying to forget. Thank heavens he was gone, she tried to tell herself. We're all better off.

She clung to that thought all day Thursday and Friday, while the drought tightened its grip on the country's breadbasket. Think about the drought, she commanded herself whenever thoughts of Nick popped into her mind. And lord knew the drought should have been enough to occupy anyone's thoughts.

For the rest of the week the sun beat down on the Midwestern plains, burning the topsoil into dust, bleaching the colour from trees and grass, baking the tops of stones that poked through the alarmingly shallow waters of every creek and pond. Grass and marsh fires raged throughout the state, fish began to die in the too-warm waters of their once icy lakes, and the worried eyes of every farmer searched the maddeningly empty sky for the clouds that would mean salvation.

Except in Random. Oddly enough, the farmers there didn't seem to notice. Right in the middle of the worst drought in state history, the residents forgot the fires and their dying crops and the cattle stuck in mud wallows and the hogs convulsing in the heat;

the only topic on anyone's lips was the Saturday night street dance.

It wasn't just heedlessness, Emily finally decided. It was a defence mechanism. For once, reality's picture was simply too grim to contemplate for long, and the dance was everyone's escape.

They came into her shop in droves to buy tickets, and inevitably they stopped to chat with their neighbours about who was coming, what they would wear, and whether the terrible heat would persist into the night and ruin the dancing. There was something terribly sad about their pervasive gaiety, Emily thought, perhaps because it was destined to be so fleeting.

By the end of Saturday night the dance would be over, and minds would be forced to return to serious matters—deadly serious matters upon which lives and lifestyles turned.

You were right, Nick, Emily thought as she watched them laugh and chatter and forget for a time that catastrophe was waiting in the wings. They needed this. They needed to forget, if only for a little while. How selfish I was not to see that.

Added to the torment of her introspection was the uncanny perception of a select few, like Mrs Hoeffer.

'I don't believe I've ever seen you so down in the mouth, Emily, dear,' she'd chirped, peering sympathetically over the counter on Friday. 'You must miss Nicky terribly.'

That particular sentiment had been re-peated a number of times, and Emily had been so startled by the directness of it that she had never been able to manage a reply. So. They all knew he was gone, and they were all busy feeling sorry for poor Emily. It was bad enough to have to admit to herself that his absence left a hole in her life; it was far worse to realise she was the object of everyone's pity.

By late Saturday afternoon, hundreds of hands working together had transformed a full block of Main Street into a huge, open-air ballroom. Sawdust covered the faded tar and dozens of milk cartons stuffed with wild flowers lined the pavements. Strings of tiny lights criss-crossed the street overhead, waiting for darkness to turn them into a canopy of electric stars. A makeshift bandstand had been erected in front of Herman's hardware store, and even stodgy old Albert had turned his restaurant into a pavement café, with every table moved outside.

Everyone had gone home to supper and chores before returning for the dance, and, when Emily ventured out on to the pavement before closing the shop, the street was deserted.

She sagged to the kerb in front of her shop, exhausted, and looked up and down the empty street. It was strangely quiet after the bustle of the day, and in its emptiness the town looked rather sad—like an abandoned carnival. She closed her eyes and drew the sweet, woody smell of sawdust into her lungs, wondering if it would sound as marvellous as it smelled when hundreds of dancing feet scuffed over it. It was something she would never know, because she had no intention of leaving her apartment that night.

'Looks good, doesn't it?' Mr Tollefson said suddenly from the silence behind her, making her jump.

'Martin!' She smiled over her shoulder at the tall elderly man—one of the few genuine smiles she'd worn this day. 'Shouldn't you be at home, helping Harriet get ready for the anniversary picnic tomorrow?'

He nodded solemnly, but his blue eyes twinkled from a web of laugh-lines years in the making. 'With a house full of kids and grandkids, she's got more bodies in that house than she knows what to do with right now. Thought I'd drive in and take a peek at the town before it gets all cluttered up with bodies tonight. And I wanted to thank you, too, for taking time out to deliver the roses personal today. I know how busy you've been.'

Emily's smile was wistful, remembering the look on Harriet's face when she'd taken the roses out to their farm over the lunch-hour. 'It was my pleasure, Martin. I'll bring the table arrangements out first thing in the morning. I thought they'd keep better in the shop coolers in this weather.'

Martin nodded. 'Appreciate that, Emily. Sincerely.' He pocketed his big hands in his overalls and rocked back on his heels, musing with a satisfied expression, 'The whole family together under one roof, the anniversary picnic tomorrow, and now this dance, to start it all off...almost feels like the whole town is celebrating our fifty years right along with us. Life surely can be good, can't it?'

Emily blinked up at him, managed a feeble smile, then jerked her head to look down at her tennis shoes, half-buried in the sawdust, and pressed her lips together.

A frown flickered across Martin's features, then he folded his long body into impossible angles to sit next to her on the kerb. He leaned forwards with his arms draped across his knees, his head tipped sideways to study her profile.

'Does loving Nick hurt that bad?' he asked softly, and she jerked her head to stare at him with dismayed astonishment. It was a thought she hadn't even articulated to herself, and thoughts like that were private—secret—not a matter for public discussion, and certainly not with someone she barely spoke to more than once a year.

Martin watched her thoughts track across her face, and an old pattern of lines deepened around his mouth when he smiled. 'Oh, I know it's none of my business, but I'm an old man, you know. You can't expect an old man to keep his mouth shut when he should.'

Emily blinked and pressed her lips even tighter together. 'I don't even *like* Nick Simon.'

His shock of white hair bobbed when he chuckled. 'Now, Emily, I'm not so old that I can't remember what lovesickness looks like on a girl's face.' He watched her lips purse in distaste, and then quiver, just a little. Lord, but she was Carl Swenson's daughter — locked up tighter than a drum. 'There's no shame in loving, child,' he said gently. ' 'Specially not a man like Nick. Never did know a woman who could resist that rascal once he set his mind to it.'

'Well, somehow I managed,' Emily mumbled, watching her toe dig a hole into the sawdust. 'And now he's gone. So that's that.' She jumped abruptly to her feet, brushing her hands against the front of her green overall.

As Martin peered up at her, he saw the trouble in those fine green eyes of hers, that kind of deep-down weariness that came from holding people at arm's length for too long. Sure as sunshine in July, she was hurting; and just as sure, she'd be too proud to admit it. He decided not to press the point.

'Well,' he said, pushing his hands against his knees and rising to face her, 'I sure would take it kindly if you'd save an old man a dance tonight.'

She looked down at where her fingers were twining together. 'Truth is, I don't know how to dance, Martin. I've never done it before.'

His eyes almost disappeared in a frown. Good lord. The girl must be looking thirty right in the eye, and she'd never danced before? 'Then you'll need an experienced teacher,' he said with a definite bob of his head. 'And no one's been waltzing more years than I have.'

'Actually...' Emily looked around aimlessly, biting her lip '...I wasn't even planning on coming tonight...'

'But that was before you knew you'd have a chance to dance with me, right?' His grin was impossibly infectious.

She hesitated a moment, then shook her head with a resigned smile. 'Right,' she conceded.

'Good. Now you be down here when this shindig starts, or Harriet and I will be at your door, I can promise you that. And Emily,' he put his huge, gnarled hands on her shoulders and smiled down at her like a benevolent grandfather, 'a girl should wear her prettiest dress to her first dance.' He grinned and winked at her, then turned and ambled away, whistling like a young man.

Emily stared after him with a baffled frown, feeling a little bit as if she'd been run over by one of those shiny metal milk trucks that tracked in and out of Martin's farmyard. He saw too much, that old man, and, without knowing her at all, he knew her too well.

She shook her head and went back inside, feeling strangely exposed, terribly vulnerable—but, now that she thought about it, a lot better than she had felt in days. Someone had looked beneath the surface, had seen the cracks in the strong façade she preserved so diligently—and it hadn't been as bad as she'd thought.

The muted twang of an electric guitar floated in through the open window as the band warmed up while Emily was still soaking in a cool bath. She'd argued with herself for the past two hours, deciding one minute she absolutely would not go down to that ridiculous dance, then deciding the next that she would. She'd been back and forth a dozen different times, until she'd finally realised that, if she didn't show up, Martin and Harriet Tollefson probably *would* come upstairs and drag her down. The certainty of that should have made her feel threatened, indignant—who were they to interfere in her life like that?—but, for some reason, it just made her feel...welcome.

With a resigned sigh she drained the tub, wrapped a towel around her dripping body, and padded barefoot into the bedroom. She grimaced at the pile of white eyelet cotton draped across her bed. She'd bought the dress on one of her rare trips to Minneapolis two years ago, and hadn't even cut the tags off yet.

You were in Minneapolis, her thoughts skittered away. You were in Nick's city that day, maybe within a few blocks of where he works or lives or walks, and you weren't even aware of it. She frowned immediately, distressed that he kept popping into her mind, and forced herself to concentrate on the dress.

It was a preposterously feminine thing, with a scooped neck and full, gauzy sleeves, cinched at the waist and exploding beneath into a puffy, cloudlike circle of fabric. She still didn't know what had prompted her to buy it—lord knew she had no call for such a dress in her life—and the truth was, she'd just snatched it off the rack without ever trying it on. She'd probably look like a perfect idiot in this pile of fluff, she thought as she slipped it over her head, jamming her arms impatiently into the sleeves; and if she did, she'd just tug on a pair of old jeans and——

She caught a glimpse of her reflection in the mirror, and her thoughts stopped dead and her expression froze. Like creatures with wills of their own, her hands rose in slow motion to press together beneath her chin. 'Oh,' she whispered, blinking at the mirror; and then, after what seemed like a very long time, she reached with a shaky hand for the make-up she hardly ever used.

Darkness was kind to Random, painting soft shadows on the squarish, straightforward architecture of a town that had better things to do than beautify its buildings. Most of the decorations were hidden by the press of hundreds of bodies, but the canopy of lights twinkled overhead, transforming this drab street into a fairyland, for at least one night.

It's our coming-out party, Emily thought wryly, wandering through the crowd in her white dress and low-heeled shoes. Mine and the town's. We're both decked out in all our finery, a couple of Cinderellas for a few magic hours, dressed to hide the plainness beneath.

Wouldn't Nick be surprised if he could see us now? she mused.

On impulse, she'd flicked her hair forward instead of slicking it back behind her ears, and let the wispy fringe sweep down to her brows. In a way, she'd been creating a disguise—an *alter ego* completely dissociated from the sedate woman who ran the Random flower shop. It was all right that this new person was frivolous enough to own a dress like this and wear eye make-up and little button earrings and go dancing in the street, because she didn't have anything to do with the real Emily at all.

She felt comfortable for her first few minutes in the crowd, almost smug in her marvellous disguise as she greeted the people she knew and marvelled at how many she didn't. But then she began to notice the quality and duration of their unabashed stares, and her confidence faltered.

Too much eyeshadow, she worried, remembering how intensely green her eyes had looked in the mirror. Or maybe the lipstick is too bright, or maybe my mascara is running down my cheeks and I've got a horn growing out of my forehead.

With every step she took down the pavement, a new pair of eyes brushed over her, then jerked back to look again. At first she just smiled and nodded politely, pretending it didn't bother her at all; but after a time she began to feel as if she were some sort of alien species, walking a gauntlet so the locals could stare with gape-mouthed wonder at the oddity. Her head dropped and she scowled at the pavement, wishing she were back in the security of her empty apartment where no one could see and secretly laugh at the spectacle of Emily Swenson pretending to be something she wasn't. She was just about to duck into the flower shop and flee upstairs when the sound of the band's first chord exploded over the murmur of the crowd and shattered the night air.

Traditionally, every dance in the farming towns of the Midwest began with a rousing polka, and this one was no exception. Emily paused to watch the first farmer tug his plump, blushing wife out on to the sawdust, and wondered how long they would be out there alone, moving in awkward, embarrassed circles before a few others moved tentatively to join them.

It took about two seconds.

Emily blinked hard at the throng of laughing couples spilling immediately out on to the street. For the most part, the first wave looked like an invasion of the elderly — white-haired men with sunburned bald spots and eyes permanently squinted from years in the sun, rosy-cheeked wives who looked better suited to needlepoint and vegetable gardening than cavorting on a makeshift dance-floor. Stiff new overalls and crisply starched shirts spilled into the street with Paisley dresses and sturdy block-heeled shoes, and they all danced. Lord, how they danced, as if they hadn't a care in the world; as if they were all happily caught in those precious years before the young come to realise that life is hard and the world is a sobering place.

Emily gaped at the sight of people she'd always thought of as old and stooped swirling with a grace and fluidity of motion that seemed gay and almost choreographed. Spinning skirts and bobbing grey-haired heads mocked the infirmities of age with the abandon of youthful spirit, and Emily found it hard to believe that these sprightly figures were the same ones who had bounced on tractor seats for years, and now spent most evenings on porch rocking-chairs.

The town should never have stopped having these dances, she caught herself thinking. It was almost as if Random had gone to sleep, as if the spark of life had mysteriously abandoned the town, leaving it old and lifeless and without spirit. The description she'd formed in her mind made her frown, because it was too close to a description of herself.

This was her first introduction to the playful side of all the stalwart people she had known since her youth; the first confirmation of that old myth that farmers loved two things almost to distraction—the land, and the dance.

She saw her own bemused expression reflected on the faces of teenage bystanders who, like Emily, had never seen their parents and grandparents kick up their heels, and then someone began to clap in time, and the street rocked with the sound of hands coming together to music that seemed to match the beat of her heart.

Before long the young people joined in, spinning in awkward imitation of the practised moves of their elders, too impatient to wait for the rock and roll the band would play later. As Emily watched the melding of generations, she forgot that she had once thought the idea of a dance silly, and wondered why the custom had died, why it had taken a man from the city to bring it to life again.

Look at those faces, she thought, her toe unconsciously tapping the beat. Not a troubled frown among them, not a single furrowed brow, and as long as this night lasts there *is* no drought, no hardship, no misery. Almost unwittingly, her hands moved to keep time and her lips curved in a smile.

He should be here, she thought suddenly, and her hands slowed, then stopped, and her smile faded. The truth was that Nick had given this night to these people, and, no matter how badly things had ended up between them, it was too bad he couldn't have stayed long enough to see the measure of joy he'd left behind.

Her shoulders slumped with the force of her sigh, and for a moment she stood staring sadly at the dancers, wondering how much the gaiety on the street would have been multiplied with the catalyst of Nick's irrepressible personality.

'I don't think I ever saw anyone look so miserable in my life. What's the matter, Emily? Can't you stand watching other people have a good time?' a voice said behind her, and her hand flew to her chest to see if her heart had really stopped, or if it had only felt that way. There wasn't another voice quite like that in the world.

She didn't really hear the words or the sarcastic delivery, only the voice, and for once in her life she never thought to hide what she was feeling, to put on the rigid mask of indifferent stoicism she had worn for so long. She just spun to face him with her breath caught in her throat and her heart in her eyes, because he'd come back, and she didn't care why, and she didn't care for how long, she just...

The joy fell away when she looked up into the hard, expressionless face. For brief moments in the past two weeks she had seen his grin fade and the blue eyes grow serious, but never had she seen him look so coldly indifferent.

There was no light of mischief in the blue eyes, no hint of amusement in the grim line of his mouth; and for perhaps the first time she noticed that his jaw was capable of a stubborn thrust, that the angles of his face could look harsh and unforgiving when he chose.

Her lips quivered slightly, straining for a smile, but there was something wrong about smiling at a face like that. It would be like smiling at a funeral. Her hands moved to rub at her arms, as if she were chilled. 'You came back,' she murmured stupidly.

He didn't say anything, and the longer the silence between them lasted, the more nervous she became. She finally found the courage to look up at him again, but his expression was so solemn that it was like looking into the face of a stranger. 'You look…different,' she said.

He raised one brow. 'So do you.'

He was staring at her with chilling directness, and she dropped her eyes and pressed her lips together, horribly aware of how foolish she must look in this ridiculous dress and hairstyle, with all that whorish make-up.

She frowned and plucked at the front of her skirt. There was a loose thread there, right in the fold; she didn't know how she could have missed it when she was cutting off the tags…

Even over the sound of the music and the crowd, she could hear his long sigh, as if he were letting something go. 'Do you want to dance with me, Emily?'

Her eyes shot up, horrified at the prospect of stumbling around through the sawdust to the fast, frantic rhythm of the polka. 'No!'

His head moved in a silent, humourless chuckle. 'I didn't think you did.' And then he turned his back and strode quickly away before she could explain.

She stood there with a dismayed expression, wanting desperately to call out, 'Wait!' but somehow unable to force out that single syllable—that one word that would acknowledge all the yearning, all the need, all that dreadfully human weakness that she had managed to lock inside for so long.

'Go after him, dear.'

Emily turned to see her mother standing next to her, her smile gentle, her eyes soft and incredibly wise.

CHAPTER TEN

'GO AFTER him,' her mother had said, and Emily's mind had immediately flashed back to when Nick had told her, 'Just ask me to stay.' Such simple phrases, both; but so hard, so damned hard to execute. How did you erase a lifetime of thinking a certain way, and just jump into a new personality as if it were a new pair of jeans? And did she really want to? Was she ready to give up her prized independence with the utterance of a single sentence, or with the blatant pursuit of a man who by his own admission wanted nothing more than an hour of pleasure?

'Your heart's all over your face,' her mother persisted. 'Go and tell him, Emily. Go and tell him how you feel.'

Lord, it wasn't just Martin Tollefson who could see the truth. It was her mother, too; and Mrs Hoeffer, and probably everyone else in the town. The mask hadn't just slipped; it had shattered into a million irretrievable pieces, and if she didn't correct that soon she'd be an object of pity for the rest of her life.

With a concentrated effort, she immediately donned an artificially bright, couldn't-care-less expression. Seeing it, recognising the stubborn, prideful look she'd seen on her husband's face a thousand times, her mother sighed and walked away, and Emily closed her eyes briefly in relief.

If there was a woman Nick *didn't* dance with that night, it wasn't for lack of trying. Every time Emily saw him he was swirling a new partner in his arms, each one gazing up at him more raptly than the last.

She'd clamped down hard on that first awful impulse to flee to the solitude of her apartment, to wallow there in self-pity and might-have-beens. But with each new woman that Nick swept into his arms it became easier to stay at the dance; she was determined to show him he couldn't hurt her—that she couldn't be hurt, full stop—because she just didn't care.

As the night wore on, maintaining the pretence of nonchalance became more and more of a strain. She strolled along the pavement, initiating conversations with startled people who had never known Emily Swenson to be so sociable; but, whatever the subject matter, it was never interesting enough to keep her eyes from straying back to the street, back to the one fair head that was taller than most of the others. She tried to concentrate on the other dancers—Martin and Harriet Tollefson in a vigorous, foot-stomping csárdás; Mrs Hoeffer blushing and tittering as an elegant-looking man from the next township waltzed her around—but inevitably her gaze would shift and sharpen on Nick and his current partner.

At one point her mother tugged her father out on to the street, and that, at least, was novelty enough to capture and hold her attention for the duration of the complex dance they executed. Afterwards her mother joined her while her father went to fetch soft drinks, and this time Emily's smile was genuine. 'You two looked like a couple of kids out there,' she told her.

Mary Swenson laughed modestly and fanned her flushed face with one hand. 'We haven't danced in years,' she mused happily. 'It's how I first fell in love with your father, you know. At a barn dance. He just swooped in on me from out of nowhere, a complete stranger, swept me out on to the floor...' She raised her eyes and exhaled with a smile, remembering. 'He never said a single word during that whole dance, but by the time it was over I knew I wanted to feel what I'd felt in his arms for the rest of my life.' She looked up at her tall, lovely daughter a little sheepishly. 'Those were pretty disgraceful feelings for a woman in those days,' she admitted wryly, 'and I was ashamed of them for a long time. It took years before I understood that the physical and the mental things were all connected. My body knew your father was the right man instantly. It took my mind a little longer.'

Emily just blinked at her in astonishment.

'Oh, dear.' Mary tried to suppress a little smile. 'Your old mother's shocked you, hasn't she?'

Emily licked her lips and swallowed, uncomfortable at sharing this extraordinarily intimate view of her mother's feelings for her father.

'When you look at Nick,' her mother continued softly, 'I can see myself, thirty years ago, in your face. I think Nick must make you feel the way your father made me feel, and oh, Emily, if he can do that, don't let him get away.'

Emily took a deep breath and scowled. 'I don't want to feel that way, Mother. It's——'

'Demeaning?' her mother interrupted with a wry smile. 'Don't look so surprised, dear. I know that's the way you've always thought of me—some poor, downtrodden, weak-willed woman, bowing to her husband's whims all the time.' She shook her head and chuckled. 'What you never understood,

Emily, is that subservience isn't an external condition. It's a state of mind. It only exists in here.' She tapped one finger to her head. 'I give to your father because it makes *me* happy, not him. Loving isn't a selfless thing, you know—a sacrifice only weak people make—it's really the most selfish act of all, and sometimes, I think, the most courageous.'

Mary smiled gently at her daughter's troubled expression, then looked back to the dancers. 'Look at that Nick,' she murmured. 'Who could blame you for falling in love with a man like that?'

A little stunned by the depth of her mother's philosophising, Emily forgot to deny loving Nick, and shifted her gaze to the street. Her gaze hardened and her mouth compressed at the sight of Nick's arms around a particularly voluptuous redhead.

'Handsome, isn't he?'

'If you like the type,' Emily replied, her voice sullen, and her mother just smiled.

It was amazing, really, that a man with such a powerful physique could move so gracefully, so effortlessly, lending an almost formal elegance to a street covered with sawdust and filled with farmers.

He was wearing a white shirt over snug, faded jeans, and every time his legs moved the delineation of long, hard musculature rose against the fabric. Broad, tanned forearms poked out of the rolled-up sleeves, looking massive and powerful as they tightened around the woman's waspish waist. She was saying something to him now, and his teeth flashed whitely in a slow, lazy smile.

'He certainly seems to be *her* type,' Emily's mother pointed out.

Emily's eyes narrowed in irritation. Just then the music stopped, and the band leader announced a full set of waltzes.

'Emily!'

She followed the voice to see Martin Tollefson lumbering towards her, his hand outstretched.

'Come on, darlin'.' He tucked her hand in the crook of his elbow and led her out on to the street. 'Harriet's just about tuckered out, and it's time for your first lesson.'

If she could have done it unobtrusively, Emily would have dragged her heels, pulling against Martin's grip, and steadfastly refused to go out there and make a fool of herself. But at the last minute she caught Nick's eyes on her, so she just smiled bravely and let Martin lead her away to her doom.

Through the clenched teeth of her smile she admitted the truth. Martin seemed to know everything there was to know about her already; what was one more weakness? 'I don't know how to do this, Martin,' she confided in a shaky whisper. 'I'm going to make a fool of myself, and everybody's looking at me. They're going to laugh.'

Martin stopped in front of the bandstand and turned her gently, nestling her in the perfect cradle of a gentlemanly embrace. 'Of course they're all looking at you,' he whispered back with a smile, blue eyes twinkling. 'You look like a fairy princess tonight, and you're breaking hearts all around.'

She was so stunned at the sheer impossibility of what he said that she barely noticed when the music started, was hardly aware of her feet automatically following his in a slow, elegant pattern that felt somehow like floating.

'That's it.' He nodded down at her with approval. 'I'll dance, you come along for the ride. Feels good, doesn't it?'

'Yes,' she agreed, amazed.

So this was dancing, she marvelled as they turned in wonderful, graceful arcs that made the lights overhead blur in streaks across the night sky. She could feel the swirl of her skirt spinning away from her legs, the soft rush of warm air against her cheeks, the strange weightlessness of her limbs.

Martin guided her with the gentle pressure of his hand on her back, the smallest tug of the hand that held hers, and just when she was beginning to feel that she could dance like this forever he stopped abruptly and, with a gracious nod, relinquished her hand to a tall, dark man who had tapped him on the shoulder.

Before Emily had a chance to protest, she was swirled away from Martin in the arms of a stranger, but he had a pleasant smile and warm brown eyes, and his hands and feet were every bit as expert as Martin's had been, and Emily found herself laughing for the sheer pleasure of it.

She danced every waltz in the set: two in a row with the man with warm brown eyes, one with Herman, who surprised her by moving his bulk with considerable agility, one with an angry-looking black-haired man whose eyes drilled hers with such intensity that he almost frightened her, and the last with Martin again, who teased her about being fickle, she changed partners so often.

'I didn't realise there were this many men in the county,' she laughed breathlessly, trying to sneak a peek over his shoulder at where Nick was dancing with the redhead—again. 'I feel like Cinderella at her first ball.'

Martin turned her smoothly—almost intentionally, it seemed—until she couldn't see Nick and was forced to look up into his own kindly face. 'You having trouble keeping your eye on the prince, Cinderella?' he asked with a gentle smile.

An indignant denial sprang to her lips, then died there, and she dropped her eyes. Fortunately, the set ended and Harriet reclaimed him before he could say anything else.

Emily joined her parents during the break, trying not to notice Nick and the redhead at one of the beer booths, standing so closely together that light couldn't find a space between them. At one point the woman reached up to slip long-nailed fingers into his hair, then pulled his head down to whisper in his ear. Her nails were painted a vibrant red, and from a distance they looked like drops of blood against the lightness of his hair. He laughed at whatever she said, then his eyes met Emily's over the redhead's shoulder, narrowed slightly, and his smile faded. She looked away quickly, but not quickly enough. The next time she glanced casually in his direction, he was leaning back against the booth, his elbows propped on the ledge, smiling insolently at her. You can't take your eyes off me, his expression seemed to say, and from that moment on she determined to do precisely that.

For the rest of the evening she was witty, she was gay, and, above all, she was gregarious, dancing whenever she was asked, flirting awkwardly with every man who took her into his arms, because flirting was as novel an experience as dancing, and Emily hadn't perfected the art yet. Still, the disguise she had hoped for at the beginning of the evening was complete, and so comfortable, in fact, that she began to wonder if it was really a disguise at all. Maybe this gay, laughing, exceedingly feminine persona had been lurking inside all along, somewhere deep beneath the years of stern features and plain clothes.

Emily felt Nick's eyes on her more than once, and, although she made a point not to seek him out in the crowd, there were times when he passed into her line of sight as they danced with their respective partners. Those moments left flashing images burned into her mind—his broad hand splayed across another woman's back, the line of his jaw shadowing his neck, the damp tumble of darkening blond spilling over his brow.

She'd just finished perhaps her fifth dance with the man with the brown eyes when she felt a hot, rough hand come down on her shoulder from behind.

'You don't mind, do you?' Nick said to the man, and, although his mouth smiled, something in his eyes stated clearly that his question was not a request.

Before the man had had a chance to declare whether he minded or not, Nick had turned Emily to face him, and his hand pressed hot and wide across the small of her back. Although it felt as if it were burning through the thin cotton fabric of her dress, his hand didn't jerk her towards him; the pressure was light, implying strength rather than executing it, and somehow that was more powerful a force.

'Emily.'

He didn't have to say any more than that. She knew what he wanted. Her eyes lifted slowly to his, then flinched slightly, as if they had encountered a brief flash of blinding light. While his eyes held hers in a smouldering blue gaze, his left hand found her right shoulder, slid slowly down her arm to her hand, then twined its fingers through hers.

'The last songs of the night are always slow dances.' His voice was a faint rumble of deep-throated thunder, and his breath stirred the hair on her forehead. 'They're supposed to cool us down...' his mouth curved in a deadly smile '...or heat us up, as the case may be.'

She felt the muscles of her neck straining as she looked up at him.

'Put your hand on my shoulder, Emily.'

Her hand moved to obey him with a will of its own, and when the music started her legs moved as well, following his lead, although she couldn't remember telling them to do that.

He didn't dance like anyone else. As a matter of fact, whatever it was they were doing didn't feel like dancing at all. There was no sensation of gliding or flying, no lifting of the spirit to soar free. It was something much more primitive than that, something that bordered on eroticism. Surely the band was playing a song? Surely there must be a melody? But if there was, Emily couldn't hear it. She could barely hear anything. Her consciousness was fixed on the throbbing beat of the drum, the strident, demanding rhythm that pumped like the heart of a huge animal.

Their bodies never touched, save for the contact-points of their hands, and yet never had Emily been so physically aware of him. She didn't have to look to see that his shirt clung damply to the rippling muscles of his stomach; she *knew*. She didn't have to see the hand on her back to know how dark his skin would appear against her dress. Somehow these things were evident in his eyes; eyes that seemed to bore into hers, screaming silently something beyond articulation, something meant only to be felt, and never spoken aloud.

She had read somewhere that dance was the most stimulating foreplay of all, and now she believed it. Blind and deaf and mindless, her body followed the movements of his with a surety and trust that was pure instinct, and in one stunning flash of revelation she understood that the dance was a microcosm of life itself, the way Nature had intended it to be. The man led, and the woman followed; the man protected, and the woman trusted, and, as abhorrent as such a concept might have been in twentieth-century conversation, in the dance, at least, it was still the essence of desire.

She wanted to be closer. Her eyelids fluttered at the thought of the power of the arm at her waist, and she wanted to feel that power pulling her towards him. Unconsciously her body moved towards his, and unobtrusively, but unmistakably, he kept her at arm's length. But his eyes shot sparks of blue, as if they had suddenly caught fire.

'Don't,' he warned her, and the hoarseness of his voice made her catch her breath audibly. He winced at the sound, then gritted his teeth and drew their locked hands up to rest on his chest.

It was just a little thing; a natural position for dancers. Emily had seen a dozen couples doing the same, but she had never imagined that it would feel like this.

His chest was rock-solid under her hand, and the wonder of the sensation made her spread her fingers and press her palm against him. Muscles jerked under her touch, and it was like holding her hand on a furnace that got hotter and hotter without burning, a furnace that expanded and contracted, faster and faster, as the beat of something that lived inside pounded against her flesh.

Her lips parted unconsciously, and she saw his gaze lash at her mouth like a whip that struck and retracted quickly.

'Emily...' He sucked her name in through his teeth, and the hand on her back jerked convulsively. For a full four steps of a dance she was no longer aware of performing, he kept his eyes closed. They were hard with determination when he opened them again.

'Who was the man you were dancing with?' he demanded in a low growl.

She frowned, mis-stepped for the first time, and struggled to make the awesome shift from sensory input to lucid thought. Had she danced with another man? Yes, of course she had...Martin, and then the brown-eyed man...what had he said his name was?

'Michael,' she remembered suddenly. 'Michael, from Dakota County...' Why did he want to know this?

His brows raised slightly, and his eyes looked suddenly icy as they raked her face. 'Don't dance with him again,' he warned her. 'He's more than you bargained for.' And then in a blatantly sensual gesture he took his hand from her back and circled her bare neck, pressing his thumb ever so slightly into the pulse in the hollow of her throat. Her heartbeat quickened, and she couldn't seem to catch her breath.

'I won't come to you again, Emily,' he said in a low tone, his eyes fixed on hers. 'You'll have to come to me.'

Dazed, she watched him walk purposefully away through the crowd of dancers, a little surprised to find that his shoulder was no longer beneath her fingers. It was only then that she realised the song was over.

'Last dance!' the bandleader called through the microphone, and before she had completely regained her senses, the black-haired man whose eyes had disturbed her was at her side, lifting her hand in his, circling her waist with his arm.

He had never uttered a word the first and only time they had danced together, and he said nothing now, just swept her close and began to move languorously to the plaintive melody of the last song. Something about the way he looked at her made her want to pull away, but she caught a glimpse of Michael moving in her direction and changed her mind. She smiled apologetically at the kind brown eyes, puzzled that Nick would warn her about dancing with him again, but none the less compelled to heed his warning. He was a man, after all, and she was totally without experience. He would know about such things. But why had he left her at all? Why hadn't he stayed to dance the last dance with her?

In a sudden, uncomfortable tug, she was swirled around until she could see Nick lounging against the beer booth, watching her intently. For some unaccountable reason, his eyes looked murderous. Just before the black-haired man spun her away, Nick raised a glass of beer towards her in an insolent, angry salute, then tipped it to his mouth.

She frowned in confusion as she was swirled away through the crowd, so baffled by his attitude that she didn't notice the tension in the arm tightening around her waist.

A few seconds later her apparently skilled partner bumped them into another couple, and he jerked her against his chest to pull her out of the way. She gasped at the surprising impact, then laughed nervously.

The next time she saw Nick, he had both hands on the redhead's waist and the woman was flattened against his body, her hips gyrating slowly in a motion that made Emily blush just to see it. His cheek was pressed to the side of that wild red hair, but his eyes were fixed on Emily, demanding that she look, and see, and understand what was going on.

The colour brightened in her face and her green eyes flashed, and when the black-haired man felt her tense he pulled her even closer, until his belt buckle pressed into the soft flesh of her stomach. She shot a hard, brittle smile at Nick, and she didn't pull away.

CHAPTER ELEVEN

ALTHOUGH the out-of-towners slipped into the darkness almost before the last chord had faded away, the people of Random lingered, clearly reluctant to see the evening end. They milled about in the street and on the pavements, chatting with friends and neighbours, almost comical in their common desire not to go home just yet.

But the magic was gone for Emily. The moment Nick had walked away from her the night had become old and tired, and she felt like a wilting flower drooping on its stem. Cinderella, indeed, she thought miserably. At least Cinderella had had enough sense to leave the ball before the spell had worn off. She, on the other hand, had stayed too long, until she was physically exhausted and emotionally drained, and, to make matters worse, she imagined she could still feel the clammy imprint of the black-haired man's hand on her back. All she wanted now was to be up in her apartment, out of her dress and shoes and under the stinging pellets of a cool shower.

She was close to the row of food and drink booths, ready to make good her escape, when Nick caught her eye.

He was standing in front of the beer booth again, just a few yards away. The redhead was still at his side, gazing up at him with blatant sensuality.

Emily felt her face grow hot, and snapped her gaze back to Nick in what she hoped was a glance of disdain. The moment their eyes met, the noise seemed to fade into the background, and the press of bodies around her seemed to vanish, and the only thing Emily could be sure really existed was the invisible thread that connected blue eyes to green.

She felt her heart thud against the wall of her chest as their gazes met and seemed to melt together; and then, with brutal intention and a grin that was almost malicious, he raised his arm and draped it around the redhead's shoulders.

Emily blinked once, her face blank, then turned sharply on her heel and walked away. She made her way through the noisy crowd to the pavement, then, simply because she was headed in that direction and couldn't seem to stop, she walked all the way around the block to the dark alley that ran behind her shop, instead of entering through the front door.

The sounds from the street were muted back here, lending a surreal sense of isolation. There was life and laughter and light just half a block away, but here, in the narrow, shadowed alley, Emily was alone. In a way, it seemed like a frozen moment from all the years of her life. People had always been there, just a short distance away, and yet by her own choice she had always been alone. It had never bothered her before. The pride of independence, the haughty sense of superiority that came from knowing you didn't need anyone—those things had always been enough to sustain her. But suddenly they weren't any more, and she didn't know how to deal with the despair.

She walked with her head down, her hands clenched behind her back, her dress and shoes the only spots of light in the black passageway.

By the time she was halfway to her back door she could hear the crowd beginning to dissipate. Truck and car doors slammed shut and engines rumbled to life, and the night was filled with sporadic calls of farewell. When she paused at her back door and fumbled in her pocket for the key, the town was already settling into its customary silence.

'Dammit, where *is* it?' she muttered, digging furiously into the one deep pocket that seemed to plunge all the way down to the hem of her dress. She stretched the mouth of the pocket wide and peered into its depths, but away from the Main Street lights she could barely see her hands, let alone the glint of silver deep in a shadowed pocket.

'Let me help you,' a deep voice rasped suddenly from behind her, and her heart jumped into her throat as she spun around, green eyes wide. 'Sorry.' But the voice didn't sound sorry. It sounded smug. 'Didn't mean to scare you.'

Emily's pulse fluttered at the sinister shadows painting holes on his face. His eyes looked black in their deep hollows, and she scrambled backwards without thinking until her spine pressed against the door. 'What...what are you doing back here?' she whispered, her voice as breathless as if she'd just run a mile. It was the black-haired man, the man with disturbing eyes and a face she had thought looked angry.

He didn't reply, but in the darkness, just before his hands snatched out to imprison her wrists, she saw the white flash of his teeth.

'Don't!' she tried to scream, but it came out as a whimper she could barely hear herself, and before she could say anything else his mouth was grinding against hers and the full weight of his body had fallen against her, pinning her to the door.

Every muscle in her body froze instantly into immobility. It wasn't happening. This simply wasn't happening. She would just stand here perfectly still and hold her breath and pretend that she wasn't being mauled, and soon this man would simply vaporise into thin air, like the bad dream he really was.

The delusion lasted for the space of a second, then her thoughts raced screaming through her mind, stirring all her frozen muscles to action. With a mighty thrust born of panic she used her body like a whip, flinging him backwards and away, and opened her mouth to scream for help.

The scream died in her throat when she saw the bewildered tip of his head, his unsteadiness as he stumbled backwards and spread his legs quickly to keep from falling.

'Wha...?' he mumbled in drunken confusion. She smelled the malty odour of beer on his breath, and heard a baffled apology in his tone when he spoke. Harmless—her mind registered the thought as she released a shaky sigh of relief. 'Hey lady, take it easy.' He raised his palms defensively. 'You don' wanna play, just say no. Don' have to tell me twice, no sir...'

All the air whooshed out of him as something dark and huge exploded into his side and knocked him a full three feet down the alleyway before he fell to the ground.

Emily jumped back in alarm and flattened herself against the door, and it was only when she saw the black-haired man jerked to his feet like an empty sack and slammed against the brick side of the building that she realised the huge dark shape had been Nick.

'No!' she cried out as she saw his fist draw back and hesitate before driving towards the man's face. 'Stop it, Nick!' He jerked his head towards her, and the illumination of a street light a block away reflected in the whites of his eyes. 'No.' She shook her head rapidly until it felt as if her brains were rattling inside her skull. 'He's drunk. He didn't mean any harm . . . he was just leaving.'

Nick's eyes disappeared in the darkness as they narrowed, but his fist quivered in the light as he held it in check. He glared at Emily, then jerked his head to look at the bleary, startled eyes of the man he held pinned against the wall.

'Nick,' Emily said quietly, her heart pounding in her chest.

His fist lowered ever so slowly, but both hands remained clenched at his sides and he hunched towards the man in a threatening posture. 'Get the hell out of here,' he said in a low, shaky voice, and the man demonstrated that he didn't indeed need to be told anything twice. He scrambled sideways away from Nick, his back against the wall, his posture defensive until he was out of range. Then he turned and staggered away down the alley, muttering under his breath. Long after he'd disappeared into the darkness, they could hear the desperate stumbling of his shoes against the tar, and then, at last, it was perfectly quiet.

Emily was still pressed back against the door, more shaken by the extraordinary sight of perpetually pleasant Nick turned violent than she had been by the man's unexpected assault. Her legs felt like columns of jelly, with only her locked knees keeping her from crumbling to the ground in a heap.

Nick hadn't moved, hadn't even turned his head towards her. 'I told you to stay away from him,' his voice lashed out at her.

She closed her eyes and pressed her lips together hard, suddenly on the defensive. 'You told me to stay away from Michael, not him!'

There was complete silence for a moment as his head rolled slowly to face her. 'I don't know who the hell Michael is, but that was the creep I was warning you about. He didn't take his eyes off you all night, and an idiot could have seen what he had in mind.' He hesitated, then his shoulders rose and fell in a silent sigh. 'He didn't hurt you, did he?' he asked gruffly.

Emily smiled bitterly in the dark. How ironic, she thought. In all of her twenty-seven years, she'd been kissed by two men, and now the only one who had the power to hurt her—who *had* hurt her—was standing here worrying that the other one had.

'No,' she said quietly. 'He didn't hurt me.'

Nick cocked his head, listening to something different in her voice, then walked to stand within a few inches of her.

She could see his features now—the heat-dampened strands of blond clinging to his forehead; the worried tilt of his brows; the masculine cut of his mouth. 'Are you sure you're OK, Em?' He brushed the backs of his curled fingers against her cheek in a heart-breakingly tender gesture.

She nodded silently, her eyes falling closed at his touch.

Oh, lord forgive her, it was all she wanted right now, just to feel his touch on her skin; *his* touch, she realised with a start, and no other. For reasons she didn't understand, it was through him that she felt connected to the rest of the world, as if he were the only gateway to a place she had never been. She needed that connection desperately, and if that need was a damning weakness, then let her be damned. Is that what love is? she wondered absently. Is it really a gut feeling—an instinctive sense of rightness that overrides everything your rational mind decrees?

'Come on, Em, let's get you upstairs.'

She nodded mutely, then turned for the door. The key that had been so elusive just moments before seemed to leap from her pocket into her hand, and she inserted it into the lock. She heard him close the alleyway door firmly behind them, then heard his steps follow her carefully through the darkened workroom, up the black, narrow stairway, and then all she could hear was the anticipatory pounding of her heart.

It wasn't exactly the way she'd pictured it, in those rare moments when she'd ever imagined herself with a man at all. No flowers, no courtship, no heartfelt declarations of love...no date for the spring prom, she added with a wry smile. Her chance at those things was long past, and this was what was left. A long walk up a dark stairway, a silent man behind her who had never promised anything more than that with him she would feel like a woman.

And that, she realised, was the most staggering promise of all. It was enough.

At the top of the stairs she turned to face him without turning on the lights. He was little more than a larger, denser shadow in a room of shadows.

'I think I'll have a little wine,' she said, and she didn't know if she said it because she'd heard it in a film, or read it in a book, or if she really needed the time and the numbing relaxation that drinking a glass of wine might offer.

'Good idea.'

The light from the refrigerator painted an eerie yellow stripe across the kitchen floor. It was all the light she needed to find two glasses and fill them from the bottle of white wine lying on its side next to the milk cartons.

Her hand shook a little as she poured, and she wondered if she would ever look back on this night with regret. He would not tell her he loved her—he had never pretended that—and now she was quietly surprised to understand how very unimportant that was. Love was not a bargaining tool, and it couldn't be withheld until you were certain of an equal return. It was just something you gave. Unconditionally. And, surprisingly, there was a sense of pride in being able to do that; in finding the courage to give love without a guarantee that you would get it back.

She carried the wine back into the dark living-room, her hands now so steady that the liquid barely moved in the glasses.

'Nick?'

She stopped just inside the doorway, sensing a new sort of quiet in the dark apartment. 'Nick?'

Nothing.

Emily didn't move for what seemed a very long time, and then very slowly, as if she paid for each motion with excruciating pain, she walked to the coffee-table, set down the glasses, then turned on the lamp by the couch. The tiny click of the switch almost covered the sound of the alley door closing downstairs. Almost, but not quite.

CHAPTER TWELVE

EMILY stopped the motion of the old wooden rocking-chair and leaned forward a bit, squinting out of her bedroom window. Yes, it *was* getting lighter out there. It really was. Just a little.

For the first time in hours, she permitted herself a brief glance at the clock over next to her bed. Five o'clock. Thank heaven. The night was nearly over.

She leaned back against the hard wooden spindles and began to rock again, pushing the floor with her bare toes. She was clad only in a loose T-shirt and panties, but even those clung damply to her skin in the heat that even darkness hadn't been able to relieve. The white dress lay in a crumpled heap next to the chair.

Too late, too late, too late—it was the litany she had rocked to for all the hours since she

236

had found Nick gone. She had learned so much in the past twenty-four hours—about Nick, about her mother and father, about joy, about love; and mostly, about herself—and yet all the knowledge had come too late.

There was a strange quality to the lightening sky outside her window, and her brows twitched as she stared at it.

Finally she pressed her hands against the rocker arms and pushed wearily to her feet, her mind too numb to register the wispy clouds that filtered the light of dawn.

'Emily!' Her mother smiled and frowned all at the same time. She was always happy to see her daughter, of course; but an unannounced visit at noon on a Sunday was absolutely unprecedented. Something had to be wrong.

'Hi, Mom.' Emily smiled tentatively through the screen of the back door, and Mary hurried to open it.

'Well, for heaven's sake, come in, child. Surely you don't have to wait for an invitation to walk into this kitchen? Sit down while I pour you some coffee. Is something wrong at the store? Don't tell me those coolers have gone on the fritz again, not in this heat! Your father's in the barn, of course, but if you need him——'

'Mom.' Emily caught her hand just as she was about to bustle away to the stove, and held her still. 'Relax. There's nothing wrong. I just wanted to see you, that's all.'

Mary smiled uncertainly, searching her daughter's face, trying to pin-point what it was that made her look so different today. Her hair, maybe. The short, fair strands were in total disarray, as if she'd just rubbed it dry with a towel and forgotten to comb it. In a way, it was a charmingly disordered look—but disorder, charming or not, had never been Emily's style. Nor had cut-off jeans and a baggy T-shirt that looked as it had been slept in, but she was wearing them, too.

Emily was examining her just as intently, as if she'd never seen her before. It was such a thorough inspection that Mary actually blushed as the green eyes so like her own flicked busily over her face, down the soft blue dress and crisp white apron, then back up to her face again.

For a moment it was so quiet that Mary became keenly aware of the rasp of grasshoppers out in the field, a sound so much a part of life on the Midwestern plains that she was rarely conscious of it.

'Emily.' She took her daughter's hand lightly in her own. 'What is it?'

Emily tried to shrug, tried to smile, but somehow couldn't quite manage either gesture.

'He stopped by this morning,' her mother said quietly, as if the half-smile and half-shrug had been explanation enough. 'To say goodbye.'

Emily looked down at the floor. There didn't seem to be anything to say, but her fingers tightened on her mother's hand, and she swallowed visibly.

Every muscle in Mary's face tensed as she searched her daughter's face. 'He'll be at the Tollefsons' all afternoon. He promised Martin he'd stay long enough for the anniversary party.' She hesitated for a moment, then squeezed her daughter's hand urgently. 'For goodness' sake, Emily, go and find him. Tell him,' she repeated her advice of the night before.

Emily released a prolonged sigh and looked up. 'I don't have to tell him. He knows already. He's known all along, I think. And still, he walked away.'

Mary's fine dark brows twitched in uncertainty.

Emily swallowed again and blinked rapidly and reached for her mother's other hand.

It was a perfectly astonishing thing, really, how a mother's arms could wrap around a fully grown woman and still manage to feel every bit as comforting as they had to a small child. For so many years, Emily had prided herself on not needing such comfort—strong people didn't, after all—but even if she had, the last place she would have expected to find it was here, in the arms of a woman she'd always loved, but secretly disdained for what she saw as weakness. Her father's arms would be strong—not her mother's—and yet here it was, a different kind of strength that went much deeper than size or demeanour, flowing into her, then back into her mother, then back to her again, completing a circle.

Carl Swenson finished his morning chores and came up to the house, pulled open the back screen door, looked inside, then stopped in his tracks. In that first instant when his wife's and his daughter's faces turned towards him, he thought it might be a wise thing for him to go right back to the barn and stay there until the world was right-side-up again. In the right-side-up world Emily never popped in unexpectedly, and she sure as hell never cried. As a matter of fact, he couldn't remember ever seeing her cry, not since he'd told her when she was a tyke that crying never solved anything but being tough often did. Damn him, anyway, for burdening his own daughter with a pioneer philosophy and a stubborn set of mind that made almost any task possible—except loving. That was the hard one.

But from the look of Emily's eyes—all red and swollen and misty—she'd been doing some crying now, and a lot of it, too, if he was any judge. His glance touched his wife, and he decided that they must have made weeping a major league sport. Mary's eyes were all misty, too.

He looked long and hard at his daughter's face and felt a lump form in his throat. 'You two are sure a sight,' he said gruffly, thinking that he had never seen either one of them look quite so beautiful before.

'You're letting every fly in the county in, Carl,' Mary admonished him gently.

He let the screen door slam shut behind him, and his Adam's apple moved up, then down in his sunburned throat. 'Clouds coming in,' he said.

'Oh, thank God,' Mary murmured, jumping up from the table at the one and only announcement monumental enough to distract her from her daughter's abrupt, tardy, painful leap into womanhood. The three of them nearly jammed together in the doorway as they rushed to the back porch.

Above them, the sky was a blue-white layer of gauze, but just to the west, the tall domes of black-bellied thunderheads were rolling towards them.

Mary stood with one hand braced on the porch railing, the other shading her eyes as she looked westward. 'Rain,' she murmured, with the same reverence as if she had murmured, 'Life.'

Emily looked out over the barren field behind the barn, where corn seeds were buried in a death-trap of thirst a few inches beneath the surface. How ironic, she thought, that the rain would come the very day that Nick would leave, as if Nature wanted to balance the departure of one with the arrival of the other.

'Let's hope that's all it is,' Carl said worriedly, pulling the collar of his chambray shirt away from his neck.

The heat seemed worse than ever, lying over the land like a blanket on a corpse. The air was still; breathless.

'Listen,' Mary whispered, and they all held their breath. 'The grasshoppers have stopped.'

Emily's eyes—the greenest things for miles around—passed over the parched landscape. There was nothing quite as ominous as the Midwestern plains gone completely silent. 'The quiet before the storm' was a phrase that this land owned, and, if the depth of this particular quiet was any measure, the storm that was coming was a big one.

'Could be hail,' Carl said thoughtfully, turning to Emily. 'Best get back and protect those big windows.'

Emily nodded absently. Like every other storefront on Main Street that had lost an expensive piece of plate glass to hail, the flower shop boasted slatted wooden blinds on outside rollers. It had been a long, long time since she'd seen them all pulled down and fastened against a coming storm.

She sighed, then turned to her mother and gave her a warm, heartfelt hug. 'You two keep your eyes on the sky, and don't forget to turn on the radio,' she reminded them. When she would have pulled away, Mary's hands lingered on her shoulders and she looked her straight in the eye.

'You might think about dropping in at the Tollefsons',' she said. 'Just to wish them happy anniversary. And if you see Nick out there, you could tell him goodbye again for me.'

Emily tried to smile at her transparency, but she couldn't quite pull it off. 'I took the rest of the flower arrangements out to the Tollefsons' early this morning, Mom. I wished them happy anniversary then.' She went down the steps and began walking rapidly towards her car before her mother could say anything else, her arm lifted in a parting wave. 'Remember the radio!' she called just before she slammed the car door and started the engine.

'Damn!' Mary muttered fervently from the porch, watching the car pull out of the drive.

Carl's eyes widened at the very first curse he had ever heard pass his wife's lips.

CHAPTER THIRTEEN

EMILY switched on the car radio before she was even out of the driveway, but the gesture was born of habit more than concern. A hundred thunderstorms marched across Minnesota every spring and summer, each one a potential threat, but part of the price you paid for reaping the bounty of the plains was learning to live with the violence of Nature.

The trees that flourished in this part of country did so because they could withstand the nearly gale-force winds that were a part of every season, and the same could be said of the people, too. Nowhere in the world was the technology of storm warning more advanced—the new weather radars detected wind velocities from miles away, and could spot tornadoes almost before they began to form. That didn't stop a storm from doing its damage, of course, but it did give the people in its path the time they needed to head for the storm shelters.

Emily had her own cosy nook in the basement under the flower shop, stocked with torches and blankets and a battery-operated radio. In an average year, the warning sirens sent her down there a half a dozen times or more, and if today was to be one of those times, so be it.

The radio crackled with static as she turned the dial. Finally she found the station that broadcast weather twenty-four hours a day.

'... massive storm front moving across the plains,' the announcer was saying in a matter-of-fact tone. 'Heavy rains, golf-ball sized hail, and damaging winds have been reported in Nebraska, Kansas and Iowa. Conditions are right for the formation of tornadoes, so leave that dial right where it is, folks, and keep your eyes on the skies.'

Emily smiled a little to hear the flip, familiar warning, and then she sensed the darkness of a huge truck closing in behind her, glanced at her rear-view mirror, and her smile vanished.

'Oh, my lord,' she murmured aloud, green eyes wide, because it wasn't a truck.

She jerked her head over her shoulder to confirm what she saw, then jerked it back and squinted at Random, shimmering in the white heat of sunlight less than a mile ahead. And there *was* sunlight ahead of her, parching the fields, flashing blindingly off the metal road signs...but behind her the world was black and terrifying.

'Too fast,' she whispered, a little knot of worry forming in her stomach because those clouds had been miles away back at the farm, but now they were nearly on top of her, and she'd been travelling at sixty miles an hour. Her eyes darted to the radio when she realised that it had suddenly gone dead, and her right hand scrambled for the dial. She found the Minneapolis stations, all broadcasting warnings of the coming storm, but the local station she'd been listening to had simply vanished from the air—the station situated in a little town thirty miles to the west, she remembered, biting down on her lower lip.

She glanced over her shoulder once again, the knot in her stomach growing larger now, and her foot jammed the accelerator to the floor even before her head had turned completely around to face the front again.

There was a wall of cloud racing up behind her with terrifying speed, and it stretched as far as she could see in either direction and thousands and thousands of feet up into the sky, where it topped out in fluffy white cottonballs. It was pitch-black and perfectly flat on the bottom, skimming close to the ground, leaving only a narrow swatch of grey between it and the horizon. Any two-year-old knew that this was the type of cloud that could, and usually did spawn tornadoes, and if Emily knew one thing, she knew she didn't want to be on the highway in a car if one should suddenly spiral down.

She was going so fast by the time she reached the outskirts of the town that she had to stand on the brakes to bring the car down to a safe speed. There were a few people standing in the middle of the sawdust and clutter left from last night's dance, all facing west, watching the sky.

She pulled up to the kerb at an angle, killed the engine, then jumped from the car, her breath quickening.

The very air around her was eerie, tinged with a sickly greenish hue that made her palms sweat. Worse than that was the deathly stillness, strangely foreboding with the black cloud racing towards them. The sounds of life were strangely absent—no dogs barking, no birds chirping, not so much as the rustle of a single leaf.

As she glanced around the scattered observers for a familiar face, Emily thought that she could actually hear them all breathing, the world was so quiet.

'Herman.' She walked up to stand next to him and spoke softly. 'See anything?'

He stared intently westward, then raised one arm and pointed. 'A little wisp dangling down, over there...see it?'

Emily followed a line from his finger and saw a thready appendage of white trailing from the cloud. It was the beginning. 'Maybe it'll go back up,' she whispered, staring at it.

'Maybe,' Herman allowed, but his feet shuffled in the sawdust, and Emily heard the sounds of other feet doing the same thing, and knew they were all preparing to sprint for cover. 'One touched down, you know. Blew the Haverford radio tower all to hell.'

Emily pursed her lips, her eyes still fastened on that harmless-looking tail of white. So that was what had happened to the radio station.

'Cloud sucked it back up, though,' Herman went on in a subdued voice. 'The National Weather Service said nothing else is showing on the radar, but I don't like the looks of that little thing, do you?'

Emily opened her mouth to answer, but in the time it took for her lips to part a million other white threads shot down from the wall cloud to join those first few trail-blazers, and even from this distance they could see the tail begin to twist.

'Lord almighty, that was fast!' Herman whispered, or maybe he'd been yelling and it only sounded like a whisper, because suddenly there was a blast of sound that resembled a freight train bearing down at full speed. Within seconds, the town sirens wailed in sympathy.

Watching the massive wall cloud give birth to a tornado was spellbinding, and Emily stood rooted to the spot by morbid fascination. It was the unstoppable majesty of Nature delivering a child of incomparable destruction, and there was almost as much beauty in it as there was terror.

With horrifying speed, the twister fattened and spread where it joined the cloud, then skewered down to stab at the ground. A spiral of brownish-black climbed the white column like a barber's pole and Emily knew that the colour represented soil and trees and pieces of buildings and whatever else the tornado had sucked in with its first deadly kiss with the earth. Whipping like a snake, it raged to-wards downtown Random, and within seconds of that first ear-splitting blast of noise the wind hit Main Street like the smack of a giant fist.

It flung Emily backwards, plastering her skirt to her body, driving flying sawdust into her eyes and nose and mouth.

A meaty hand snatched at her arm, tightened around it, and hauled her towards the hardware store. Unprotesting, she let Herman drag her into the store, then rush her down the centre aisle towards the basement steps. Halfway down it occurred to her that she'd forgotten to lower the wooden blinds in front of the shop windows, but there was no question of going back outside now.

'Don't think it'll hit here,' Herman hollered over the noise that sounded like an advancing army even from inside the building, 'but it never hurts to be too careful.' He pulled a battery-powered lantern out of the dark and turned it on, then gestured towards a couple of old tattered chairs in the far corner. 'The ceiling's reinforced with concrete over there. That's where we'll wait it out.'

Emily nodded, breathless, and picked her way over to the chairs.

It was too noisy to talk for nearly five minutes, and then it was so suddenly quiet that it was hard to imagine there had even been a storm. Herman and Emily both stared up at the ceiling in silence, then glanced at each other sheepishly, like two Chicken Littles who had run for cover with no reason.

'Must have hopped clean over the town, but for a minute there it sure looked like we were going to get it,' Herman remarked, trying to justify two adults' cowering in a basement.

'It sure did,' Emily agreed with a nervous laugh. 'I never saw one that close before.'

Upstairs they found the hardware store in perfect order, quiet except for a heavy rain splattering against the windows. Outside, debris from the street dance was plastered wetly against buildings and cars, and the pavement had been swept clean of its dusty carpet of sawdust, testament to the force of the wind that had passed through. There would be branches down and scattered shingles throughout the town, and the electricity might be out for hours, but as far as Emily could see up and down the street there had been no serious damage. The colour of the world had returned to the normal dreary grey of any thunderstorm, and the store windows across the street showed other faces peering out, just like theirs.

She and Herman stood in front of the window, as still as two mannequins, watching the blessed rain pelt down.

'It was worth a scare, to get this rain,' Herman mused finally.

'Amen to that,' Emily replied.

'Still, it's too bad it couldn't have waited a few hours. Must have put a damper on the Tollefsons' picnic.' Herman shoved his hands in the pockets of his baggy trousers and rocked back and forth on his heels, studying Emily's profile out of the corner of his eye. 'You planning on going out there?'

She shook her head, still staring out at the rain.

'Nick's there, you know.'

'So I heard.'

For a time there was nothing but the sound of the rain outside, then Herman sighed dramatically. 'Says he's leaving town for good tonight.'

Emily pursed her lips and said nothing.

'Thought you might be going out there to say your goodbyes before he left.'

Emily shot a glance to her left, but Herman was still rocking, staring innocently out of the window.

'The town sure will miss him. Almost everyone wishes he'd stick around, make his home here again.'

Emily blew a sharp breath out through her nose. 'Then "almost everyone" should ask him to stay,' she said irritably.

Herman nodded sagely. 'Almost everyone has.' He let that sink in for a moment, then added, 'Except you.' He turned his head sideways to look at her, his face genuinely puzzled.

Emily just took a deep breath and ignored him.

Eventually, Herman turned back to look out of the window. The rain was slowing to one of those steady drizzles that promised to last for a long time. Suddenly his head jerked backwards in surprise as a muddy brown pick-up roared out of nowhere and screeched to a halt in front of the store, its blunt nose pointing straight towards them, rocking with the force of its stop.

Fred Larson's truck, Emily's mind recorded automatically.

A whipcord-lean man popped out of the driver's door and stood on the running-board, rain dripping from the brim of his straw hat, one hand cupped around his mouth as he yelled frantically, 'We need help out here!'

By the time Herman and Emily reached the door and yanked it open, Fred was leaning on the truck horn, filling the town with a steady, raucous blare that was somehow more frightening than the sirens had been. All up and down Main Street people were popping out of the doors of Sunday-quiet shops, running through the rain to where the pick-up had stopped, its noisy engine still racing.

'We been hit!' Fred cried, and Emily's heart seemed to plummet to her stomach. 'Touch down at the Tollefsons',' he panted, panic shortening his breath, 'and the place is damn near levelled!'

'Oh, dear lord!' was the fearful exclamation that raced through the mind of every person within earshot, and for a brief instant they all froze where they stood. That instant was a lifetime for Emily as names flashed through her thoughts with the blinding glare of a neon rollcall.

Martin. Harriet. Their children and their grandchildren.

And Nick. Oh, yes. Let's not forget about Nick.

'Anybody hurt?' Herman demanded, giving voice to the question they all wanted answered.

Fred was already clambering back into the truck, ready to race away. 'They're all trapped in the storm cellar,' he hollered through the window, 'but the house collapsed on top of 'em, and we gotta dig through.' His eyes closed briefly, as if he'd just remembered something. 'Except for one guy,' he added tightly. 'Don't know how bad he is, but there was a godawful lot of blood. Old Art Simon's boy—what's his name?'

The world seemed to go perfectly still and Emily's lips formed the name silently. Nick. His name was Nick.

'Oh, Jesus,' Herman mumbled under his breath, his eyes sagging closed for a heartbeat.

'Come on, everybody!' Fred banged the top of his truck in frustrated impatience, and the sound seemed to galvanise everyone into action. A few scrambled into the back of the pick-up, a few more inside, and the rest ran for their own vehicles.

Emily couldn't remember racing for her car. All she knew was that one minute she was standing next to Herman mouthing Nick's name, and the next she was behind the wheel, a rain-wet hand fumbling at the ignition, her heart pounding so hard it felt as if it would burst through her chest. Herman jumped in the passenger side just as her hand hit the gear lever and slammed it into gear.

'Call the sheriff!' he bellowed out of the window to someone, and then Emily's foot found the accelerator and the car leaped forward in a screeching take-off eastward out of town.

'Turn on the windscreen wipers, Emily,' Herman said with amazing calm, reaching for his seat-belt, his eyes squinting through the rivulets of water running down the glass.

Her left hand scrambled over the buttons on the dash-board while her right clutched the steering-wheel of the speeding car in a death-grip. White showed all around the green of her eyes as she stared straight ahead. 'I-can't-find-it-Herman-I-can't-find-it.' The words ran into one another desperately, breathlessly, and then Herman's hand reached over behind the steering-wheel and pulled a button, and rubber blades swept two fans shapes on to the windscreen.

The wipers thumped frantically on high speed, barely keeping up with the force of the rain. Emily's palms were sweating, and her hands felt slick on the wheel.

You shouldn't be driving, she told herself mindlessly, even as her foot pressed harder on the accelerator. You've never driven this fast in your life and there's water on the road and there could be trees down ahead and you'll never be able to stop in time and your hands keep slipping off the wheel and——

'Emily.' Herman's quiet voice shattered her thoughts. 'Slow down a little. The turn-off's just ahead.'

She lifted her foot obediently, then jerked her eyes left for just a second. Even through the rain, she could see the emptiness of a ploughed field stretching towards the horizon. 'No, not yet. You can always see the barn from the road, it's so damn big; you can see that big red barn from half a mile away, and that's when you turn——'

'Slow down, Emily,' Herman repeated in a solemn voice. 'We won't be able to see the barn.' He was leaning forwards against the strap of his seat-belt, frowning out of her side window. 'It's gone.'

The car fishtailed on the slick road when she hit the brakes, barely managed to turn on to the Tollefsons' dirt road, and it was then that they saw the first evidence that the twister had indeed touched down.

They sped past what looked like a pile of kindling stacked by a madman, and Emily remembered that only this morning it had been a thick grove of young birch. Further down the washboard road, hundred-year-old pines lay on the ground like enormous arrows, pointing the way the storm had gone, showing their plate-bottom root clusters to the road. And where there had been no trees to jerk up or topple, the tornado had cleared a quarter-mile-wide path by ripping up the earth itself and leaving the clay subsoil exposed to the rain. The path led directly to the Tollefsons' farm.

'I can't see the place,' Emily murmured, her lips strangely numb, her eyes wild.

'Wait till we round the curve,' Herman tried to reassure her, but his voice was shaky, too. 'You can never see the house till you round the curve.'

But there was no house.

Emily spun into the long driveway, mud flying from her car's back wheels, and only just managed to veer the car around the feathery top of a doomed cottonwood lying on its side. Before they were halfway up to where the house had been, her expression had become glazed. The extent of the destruction was simply too much for her mind to absorb.

Off to the left, the once massive hay barn that held ten thousand bales in a good year had been flattened like a collapsed house of cards.

Less than twenty feet away, the smaller dairy barn stood pristine and undamaged, spared by the fickle nature of a storm that hopped helter-skelter over the earth, raising hell itself in one square foot and leaving the next untouched.

But the house looked as if it had exploded from the inside, and its pieces were scattered as far as the eye could see. All that was left was a pile of rubble heaped over the foundation. Perversely, Harriet Tollefson's grandfather clock stood in the centre of the destruction that had once been their living-room, as staid and dignified as ever.

Emily and Herman leaped from the car just as the brown pick-up led a caravan of vehicles into the driveway.

'This way!' Herman cried, his stout legs pumping towards the remains of the house, the rain plastering wisps of hair to his balding crown.

A lone man was tearing through the rubble on the far side, trying to clear a path to the outside storm-cellar doors. He was incredibly tall and looked like a younger version of Martin himself—a son, perhaps, or maybe even a grandson. With her heart in her throat and the rain flattening her hair to her skull,

Emily raced after Herman, passed him, and reached the man first.

'Where's Nick?' she screamed, grabbing his arm and jerking him upright with a strength that belied the difference in their sizes.

Panic-stricken blue eyes blinked in confusion and his hands clenched and unclenched as if they were still pulling at the clutter of debris at his feet. 'I gotta get them out!' he yelled suddenly, coming to his senses, jerking away to tear at the rubble again.

'But where's Nick?' she shrieked at the top of her lungs. 'Fred said he was hurt!' But then the people from the town dived into the wreckage and pushed her aside. A hand grabbed her shoulder from behind, trying to turn her, and she pulled away furiously, but the grip was too tight and now the hand was dragging her back, further away from the only man who might know what she had to know, what her life suddenly depended on knowing, and with a rush of rage-fuelled adrenalin she spun with her eyes wild and her hands raised to shove the man aside, and then she froze.

'I'm all right, Em,' he said softly.

His hair was soaking wet, with blond strands glued to his forehead, dripping water on to the shelf of his lashes and down over cheeks that were pale beneath the tan. An ugly gash skittered over the full length of his right brow, oozing bright red blood that the rain kept trying to wash away; but his eyes were bluer than ever and his mouth quirked in a half-smile.

'It bled a lot,' he said, following her eyes to his forehead. 'Head wounds always do.'

Her lips turned inwards as her body wondered what to do with all the adrenalin rushing through her veins, then she covered her face with her hands and simply burst into tears.

'Em,' her name came out in a stunned rush of air as he reached out with both arms and drew her close, and she buried her head in his shoulder and let the tears come. She heard his soft chuckle in her ear. 'You're blowing it, Em,' he murmured. 'You know what people are going to think, if they see you crying on my shoulder like this...'

But Emily just kept crying, clinging to his upper arms, because people weren't going to think anything they didn't know already. They *all* knew, it seemed. She was the only one who hadn't.

For a moment that was over too soon, because it was where he wanted to be and what he wanted to be doing more than anything in the world, Nick stood there holding her in the rain. Then he took her shoulders in his hands, pushed her gently away and crouched a little to look directly into her eyes. 'Dammit, Emily,' he said tenderly, 'you've got a lousy sense of timing. We have to dig those people out.'

His hands left her shoulders so abruptly that she nearly fell, and it was as if his hands had kept her from remembering anything but how close she'd come to losing him. Standing there alone, she suddenly remembered Martin, Harriet, all the children. She spun and moved quickly to follow him to where

Herman was straining to lift a ceiling joist from the debris over the storm-cellar doors.

'Dam-*mit*!' Herman cried. 'It's too heavy. We need the tractor!'

Oh, lord, Emily thought as she eyed the beam in dismay. It was as thick as a man's body and a full ten feet protruded from the pile of splintered lumber and brick.

'The tractor's buried under the hay barn,' Nick shouted over the rain. 'But we don't need it; not with all these hands.' He approached the centre of the beam, bent to a squat, then slid his arms beneath it up to the elbow. He looked up at the circle of faces around him with that maddening grin of his. 'Well, come on, people. Let's get this thing out of the way.'

Every face in the circle, including Emily's, gaped at him as if he'd lost his mind.

'Nick.' Herman laid a hand on his shoulder. 'There's no way in hell we can move that thing. It's just too damn big. We'll have Fred run over to his place and bring back his tractor.'

Nick was still smiling, but Emily saw something flash in his eyes; something bright and hard and almost frightening. 'I'm not so sure we want to wait that long, Herman,' he said with forced calm. 'Not without knowing if anyone down there is hurt.'

Emily looked worriedly at the dreadful paleness of his face, the too-bright eyes, and moved quickly to crouch next to him. 'It's too big, Nick,' she whispered earnestly. 'You can't move it.'

His grin only broadened. 'Not alone, I can't. None of us can do anything very well alone, Em. Haven't you figured that out yet?'

And then he bent to the task, his head twisted to one side, his eyes screwed shut, white teeth grinding as the muscles in his arms bulged and snapped. There was something decidedly pathetic about Nick straining down there all by himself while the rest of them looked on, all resigned to the futility of it . . . but in a way, hopeless or not, his effort was a rebuke to those who wouldn't even try, and Emily actually caught herself smiling, wondering if there was anything in the world quite as unwilling to admit defeat, quite as insanely stubborn, as the son—or the daughter—of a Midwestern farmer.

Without another word, she slipped her own arms under the beam, and felt the prickle of splinters slicing into her flesh.

His eyes opened long enough to see her face straining next to his, and a defiant blue gaze met a defiant green one as they tackled their very first common enemy.

'Oh, hell,' Herman muttered, dropping to Nick's other side, and then everyone stooped to the task and the beam was cradled in a row of arms, and the sound of perfectly synchronised grunts and gasps drowned out the sound of the rain. A little time later a new sound chimed in—the agonised screeching of wood scraping across metal and concrete and glass as a small group of people defied all the laws of physics, and, working together, moved an enormous length of timber where it didn't want to go.

CHAPTER FOURTEEN

For the rest of her life Emily would carry one pictorial memory of the day the tornado hit the Tollefsons' farm—a single image so sharply etched that it crowded all the others from her mind. She would forget the dulling shock at her first sight of the destruction; she would even forget the rousing cheer when the storm doors were finally uncovered and Martin and his whole family stepped out of the cellar like a parade of phoenixes rising from the ashes—but she would remember forever what she had seen in Nick Simon during the fifteen minutes between the two events. Grim determination, a singularity of purpose, and an enormous strength of spirit—the dark, powerful forces that lived beneath the mischievous eyes and the cocky grin—things she had never seen before.

He'd worked like a madman after the beam had been pushed to one side, his blue eyes narrowed against the driving rain and his jaw grimly set, the muscles of his back and arms bulging and straining as he heaved two-by-fours and concrete blocks and pieces of furniture aside as if they were weightless. He'd been wearing the familiar black tank-top, and it had clung to his torso when he'd twisted, and sagged with its weight of moisture when he'd straightened. Sometimes his face reddened and the cords of his neck stood out sharply with effort, and sometimes, when he pressed his hands to his waist and bowed backwards for a moment, his features relaxed.

But always there was the aura of absolute invincibility about him, the sense that he was not, and perhaps had never been, a man who would surrender to circumstance, but rather, a man whose heart and spirit were every bit as strong as his body.

As she worked beside him, her vision blurring from rain and sweat, her hands scraped raw and her muscles screaming, Emily glanced at him occasionally and thought she saw ghostly images of other men—her father, stone-faced and tight-lipped as he rushed to bring the hay in before a storm; Nick's own grandfather, tall and wiry and defiant, right up to the day of his death. This land made men like that, and for the first time she realised that Nick was one of them, that he had always been one of them.

Accommodations for the entire Tollefson clan were quickly arranged, with the rescuers nearly coming to blows over who would have the privilege of putting them up. There would be a barn-raising here in the next week, Emily thought; and soon after that, a house-raising, too.

While Fred Larson waited patiently in his truck, Harriet next to him, sheltered from the rain, Martin lingered to look back on the devastation that had been his farm such a short time before. Emily and Nick stood next to him.

'It's a real mess, isn't it?' Martin clucked, shaking his head, and for a moment Emily thought she might burst into tears again, the scene around them was so awful, so hopeless. 'But by heaven,' Martin went on, his old face lifting in an incredible grin, 'isn't this just the dandiest rain you ever did see? The corn should fairly leap out of the ground after this one.' He sighed happily, and Emily's impulse to cry was gone immediately. Martin didn't need it. 'The family's OK, even the cattle are OK, and the rest . . .' He shrugged lightly, dismissing the importance of anything else. He looked down at Emily at his side, then reached over to chuck her under the chin. 'As I told you, Em, life can be so good sometimes, can't it?'

Emily shook her head a little and smiled up at him. 'You're crazy, Martin, you know that?'

He nodded soberly, then winked at her. 'Man would have to be, to be in this line of work.' Then he joined his wife in Fred's truck, and the old pick-up backed gingerly out of the muddy drive.

'He's an amazing man,' Nick said quietly as they both watched the truck pull away.

'He's a farmer.' Emily shrugged, still smiling, loving Martin Tollefson and all the men like him so hard that it hurt. She swallowed hard, then glanced over at Nick. 'You're bleeding again.'

He reached up wearily with two fingers to touch his forehead, then shrugged when they came away red.

'Maybe I should take you to the hospital.'

'I'm a doctor, remember?' he sighed. 'And it's a clean cut. One stitch, maybe two. I'll take care of it when I get home.' He looked right into her eyes, and she noticed how pale he had become, how unutterably weary the old cocky grin seemed when he tried to put it in place.

'Come on,' she said brusquely, grabbing his arm and leading him to her car. 'Home is exactly where you're going.'

'Yes, ma'am.'

By the time she pulled the car to a stop beneath the ancient cottonwoods that sheltered his grandfather's driveway, Nick was sound asleep in the passenger seat. His head was rolled towards her, and she just sat there for a moment, looking at him, reluctant to move.

Already his rain-soaked hair was drying to a blond fluff over his forehead, nearly obscuring his brows. It needs trimming, she found herself thinking. I could do that. Her hand reached automatically to smooth it back, then jerked away when his eyes fluttered open. The sky will be that colour, she thought, just as soon as these clouds pass. A pure, glistening, crystalline blue.

The rain had finally stopped, and the only sound was the car engine ticking as it cooled, and the steady drip of water from freshly washed leaves.

'Well,' he sighed, straightening in the seat and looking around. 'I could use some help with this cut. Will you come in?'

She nodded, unsmiling, and reached for the doorknob, then hesitated, her eyes focused on the house. 'I don't believe it,' she whispered, dumbfounded.

It was an enormous white frame farm-house, like a hundred others dotting the countryside, except for one thing. Barring a four-foot wide staircase that led up to the front porch, the entire building was sur-rounded by a broad flower-bed necklace of daisies. White daisies, yellow daisies, even pink daisies; hundreds of them, perhaps thousands, crammed together around the house like a magic circle.

Nick followed her gaze and smiled. 'My grandmother planted those beds, years ago,' he said. 'Grandpa said she loved daisies more than anything except him. He used to spend hours taking care of these flowers. I think they connected him to her somehow, even after she was gone.'

Emily nodded numbly as she followed Nick into the house, remembering the bright pile of daisies heaped on Art Simon's grave-site. It didn't surprise her, then, to find the in-terior of Art Simon's house almost painfully neat, yet somehow crowded with the presence of a wife who had died nearly a quarter of a century before.

As they passed through the living-room on the way to the kitchen, Nick gestured at a sideboard that held dozens of framed photographs of his grandmother. 'The shrine,' he explained with a fond shrug. 'She was never really gone, as far as he was concerned.'

They were all the same, Emily thought as she followed Nick through the house. Martin, filling his home with roses for his wife, after fifty years together; her father, so devastated at nearly losing her mother a decade ago that he still couldn't speak of that time aloud; and now Art Simon, preserving a memory a quarter of a century old with a living tribute he'd tended every day. All strong, commanding men, all seemingly dominant over retiring, complacent wives—and yet their lives revolved around their women, began and ended with their women, and in truth no one person controlled another. Love controlled them all.

Nick turned in the kitchen doorway to face her, and Emily had to stop quickly to avoid running into his chest. 'I'm going to shower, clean this cut, then stitch it up now,' he said.

'I thought you wanted me to help.'

He stared at her for a moment, his face expressionless. 'I lied.' And then without a word he left the room, and Emily knew he was leaving her the option of slipping away gracefully, without any awkward explanations.

She was sitting at the scarred wooden table when he came out, fresh coffee in the pot, a mug steaming in her hands. She looked up when he paused in the doorway and stared at him.

He wore fresh jeans and a clean white T-shirt. His hair was damp and tangled, pushed up and away from the two neat black stiches over his brow. The area around the cut was rapidly turning an angry purple colour, making the rest of his face appear pale and his eyes shockingly blue.

'You're still here,' he said softly, hunching his shoulders and leaning sideways against the door-jamb.

She looked straight at him, her face expressionless, saying everything she wanted to say in a single word. 'Yes.'

He hadn't been moving, but it still seemed that he had suddenly jerked to a halt. 'Em...' he began, then he frowned hard at her, clamped his mouth closed, and walked over to stand behind her chair.

She couldn't see him, but she didn't have to. She imagined what he looked like, standing tall and broad behind her, a powerful, muscular figure that dwarfed hers, wearing an expression that rendered all that power useless, that brought them to the same level.

His hands covered her shoulders almost completely, they were so large; and even while she felt the strength of those hands she felt the love that tempered that strength and made his touch gentle, almost reverent.

She felt the brush of his lips against the top of her head, then pressed her cheek into the palm cupped to receive it, her eyes falling closed. They remained like that for a long moment while he stroked her short hair with one hand and cradled her face with the other. Then slowly, inevitably, his hands moved back to her shoulders, then crept downwards until his fingers rested on the rise of her breasts. He pressed lightly into the yielding flesh, and she heard his breath catch, and imagined his eyes slamming shut. She felt the trembling of his hands through the thin cloth of her shirt, and let her head fall back to rest against his stomach. Muscles jumped and tensed where her head pressed against him, and, almost reflexively, his hands slid quickly down over her breasts to flatten against her ribcage, pulling her back against the wooden spindles of the chair.

'You left me last night,' she said quietly, and his hands stilled.

After a moment of complete silence, he spoke. 'Because you didn't ask me to stay.'

Emily took a deep, shaky breath, then added in a whisper, 'And today you're leaving Random, for good.'

His fingers tightened almost imperceptibly across her ribs, and then he said it again. 'Because you didn't ask me to stay.'

'Everyone else did.'

'I know. But you didn't.'

Her lips felt almost liquid as they moved into a smile, and for the first time she finally understood the enormous power of submission. 'Stay, Nick,' she whispered, a little surprised because the words hadn't been so hard to say after all. 'Please stay.'

Above her head, where she couldn't see it, Nick's eyes fell closed and his face tightened. He didn't move for what seemed like a very long time, then he bent his head next to hers and his rasping whisper felt like a hot wind against her neck.

'Is that what you want, Em?'

She nodded weakly, her eyes closed.

'For how long?'

'For as long as you want me,' she whispered back, and then she smiled, because it sounded like such a subservient thing to say, and yet it wasn't subservient at all, because she knew he wanted her forever. Just as her mother knew, and Harriet Tollefson, and Nick's grandmother...and all the other strong, country women who built marriages that would last a lifetime and beyond, because they weren't afraid to be women, or afraid to let their men be men.

'I'll want you forever.' He said it aloud, not realising that he didn't have to, and then he took a deep breath, removed his hands from her, and walked back to the doorway.

Emily turned in her chair to see him standing there, his jaw clenched, his blue eyes on her steadily.

'Come with me, Em,' he said quietly, as if this one last gesture had to be made. When he raised his hand towards her, it quivered slightly.

Because old habits died hard, and because there was a lingering trace of rebellious independence in her soul, she didn't immediately leap from her chair and rush into his arms. As a matter of fact, she rose very slowly, sedately enough so that the old Emily would have been proud of her, and then she walked towards the man who had called her.

It was a simple thing—just moving one foot forward, then the other, then the first again—but somehow it felt like dancing.

MILLS & BOON NOW PUBLISH
EIGHT LARGE PRINT TITLES A MONTH
THESE ARE THE EIGHT NEW TITLES
FOR SEPTEMBER 90.

———————— * ————————

PULSE OF THE HEARTLAND
by Melinda Cross

LOVE AT FIRST SIGHT
by Sandra Field

UNSPOKEN DESIRE
by Penny Jordan

DARK PURSUIT
by Charlotte Lamb

A CHRISTMAS AFFAIR
by Carole Mortimer

FORBIDDEN ATTRACTION
by Lilian Peake

AGAINST ALL ODDS
by Kay Thorpe

SEA FEVER
by Anne Weale

MILLS & BOON NOW PUBLISH
EIGHT LARGE PRINT TITLES A MONTH.
THESE ARE THE EIGHT NEW TITLES
FOR OCTOBER 90.

———————— * ————————

THE TIGER'S LAIR
by Helen Bianchin

PASSIONATE AWAKENING
by Diana Hamilton

BREAKING AWAY
by Penny Jordan

SPELLBINDING
by Charlotte Lamb

IT ALL DEPENDS ON LOVE
by Roberta Leigh

THE GIRL WITH GREEN EYES
by Betty Neels

THE LOVING TOUCH
by Catherine Spencer

THE GOLDEN THIEF
by Kate Walker

WHAT'S NEW IN LARGE PRINT?

CLASSIC LARGE PRINT

Twelve best-selling titles from
twelve best-selling authors.

Listed below are the twelve Classics currently
available through your local library:

Title	Author	ISBN
Dark Enchantment	Helen Bianchin	0 263 11848
Escape Me Never	Sara Craven	0 263 11470
With a Little Luck	Janet Dailey	0 263 11845
Loving	Penny Jordan	0 263 11846
Love in the Dark	Charlotte Lamb	0 263 11849
Too Bad to be True	Roberta Leigh	0 263 11850
Duelling Fire	Anne Mather	0 263 11426
Elusive Lover	Carole Mortimer	0 263 11471
A Summer Idyll	Betty Neels	0 263 11472
High-Country Governess	Essie Summers	0 263 11847
Double Deception	Kay Thorpe	0 263 11427
Sun Lord's Woman	Violet Winspear	0 263 11428